2

0 9/9.0.0
0.0.02
202
798

Nove
BARONE
in Bost

In addition to our regular flavors of gelato, this month we are featuring:

- **Tall, cool drink of tart lemonade**

  With her incredible legs and honey-blond hair, Claudia Barone bowled Ethan over at first sight. But the strong, sassy society dame was not about to make him forget who was in charge of this investigation. He'd match her clue for clue, kiss for kiss….

- **USDA Grade-A prime beefsteak**

  Ethan Mallory was as different from Claudia as any person on the planet. But the rough-and-tumble private eye got to her like no man ever had. Beneath his gruff exterior was a real diamond in the rough.

- **Decadent chocolate bombe**

  No longer able to resist him, Claudia gave herself over to Ethan's kisses, to his touch. Being with him was different—explosive, dizzying, mind-blowing. She'd revel in it—for as long as it lasted. After all, none of her other relationships had had any duration. But, then again, Ethan wasn't like any other man….

Buon appetito!

Dear Reader,

Thank you for choosing Silhouette Desire—where passion is guaranteed in every read. Things sure are heating up with our continuing series DYNASTIES: THE BARONES. Eileen Wilks's *With Private Eyes* is a powerful romance that helps set the stage for the daring conclusion next month. And if it's more continuing stories that you want—we have them. TEXAS CATTLEMAN'S CLUB: THE STOLEN BABY launches this month with Sara Orwig's *Entangled with a Texan.*

The wonderful Peggy Moreland is on hand to dish up her share of Texas humor and heat with *Baby, You're Mine,* the next installment of her TANNERS OF TEXAS series. Be sure to catch Peggy's Silhouette Single Title, *Tanner's Millions,* on sale January 2004. Award-winning author Jennifer Greene marks her much-anticipated return to Silhouette Desire with *Wild in the Field,* the first book in her series THE SCENT OF LAVENDER.

Also for your enjoyment this month, we offer Katherine Garbera's second book in the KING OF HEARTS series. *Cinderella's Christmas Affair* is a fabulous "it could happen to you" plot guaranteed to leave her fans extremely satisfied. And rounding out our selection of delectable stories is *Awakening Beauty* by Amy J. Fetzer, a steamy, sensational tale.

More passion to you!

Melissa Jeglinski

Melissa Jeglinski
Senior Editor, Silhouette Desire

Please address questions and book requests to:
Silhouette Reader Service
U.S.: 3010 Walden Ave., P.O. Box 1325, Buffalo, NY 14269
Canadian: P.O. Box 609, Fort Erie, Ont. L2A 5X3

With Private Eyes

EILEEN WILKS

Published by Silhouette Books
America's Publisher of Contemporary Romance

If you purchased this book without a cover you should be aware that this book is stolen property. It was reported as "unsold and destroyed" to the publisher, and neither the author nor the publisher has received any payment for this "stripped book."

This one's for Karen,
who's always willing
to listen.

Special thanks and acknowledgment
are given to Eileen Wilks for her contribution
to the DYNASTIES: THE BARONES series.

SILHOUETTE BOOKS

ISBN 0-373-76543-6

WITH PRIVATE EYES

Copyright © 2003 by Harlequin Books S.A.

All rights reserved. Except for use in any review, the reproduction or utilization of this work in whole or in part in any form by any electronic, mechanical or other means, now known or hereafter invented, including xerography, photocopying and recording, or in any information storage or retrieval system, is forbidden without the written permission of the editorial office, Silhouette Books, 233 Broadway, New York, NY 10279 U.S.A.

All characters in this book have no existence outside the imagination of the author and have no relation whatsoever to anyone bearing the same name or names. They are not even distantly inspired by any individual known or unknown to the author, and all incidents are pure invention.

This edition published by arrangement with Harlequin Books S.A.

® and TM are trademarks of Harlequin Books S.A., used under license. Trademarks indicated with ® are registered in the United States Patent and Trademark Office, the Canadian Trade Marks Office and in other countries.

Visit Silhouette at www.eHarlequin.com

Printed in U.S.A.

Books by Eileen Wilks

Silhouette Desire

The Loner and the Lady #1008
The Wrong Wife #1065
Cowboys Do It Best #1109
Just a Little Bit Pregnant #1134
Just a Little Bit Married? #1188
Proposition: Marriage #1239
The Pregnant Heiress #1378
**Jacob's Proposal* #1397
**Luke's Promise* #1403
**Michael's Temptation* #1409
Expecting...and in Danger #1472
With Private Eyes #1543

Silhouette Intimate Moments

The Virgin and the Outlaw #857
Midnight Cinderella #921
Midnight Promises #982
Night of No Return #1028
Her Lord Protector #1160
Midnight Choices #1210

Silhouette Books

Broken Silence
"A Matter of Duty"

*Tall, Dark & Eligible

EILEEN WILKS

is a fifth-generation Texan. Her great-great-grandmother came to Texas in a covered wagon shortly after the end of the Civil War—excuse us, the War Between the States. But she's not a full-blooded Texan. Right after another war, her Texan father fell for a Yankee woman. This obviously mismatched pair proceeded to travel to nine cities in three countries in the first twenty years of their marriage, raising two kids and innumerable dogs and cats along the way. For the next twenty years they stayed put, back home in Texas again—and still together.

Eileen figures her professional career matches her nomadic upbringing, since she's tried everything from drafting to a brief stint as a ranch hand—raising two children and any number of cats and dogs along the way. Not until she started writing did she "stay put," because that's when she knew she'd come home. Readers can write to her at P.O. Box 4612, Midland, TX 79704-4612.

DYNASTIES: THE BARONES

Meet the Barones of Boston—
an elite clan caught in a web of danger,
deceit…and desire!

Who's Who in
WITH PRIVATE EYES

Claudia Barone—She's always fixing her family's problems, but her own love life is a mess. Her former beaux never lasted longer than four months; they were too intimidated by her stubbornness and her strength….

Ethan Mallory—Despite hailing from the wrong side of the tracks, he's always been attracted to tall, cool blondes—all of whom have been Ms. Wrong. This time he tells himself he'll stay away from Ms. Barone, no matter how much it kills him….

Derrick Barone—He, more than anyone, knows you can't fight who you really are.

One

Uncle Miles had always told him his sense of humor would get him hanged one of these days, Ethan reflected. Maybe today was the day.

"I'd like to start as soon as possible." The blonde sitting on the other side of his desk gave him a bright smile. "This is going to make a terrific article."

Maybe it was his curiosity that would get him in trouble this time. As much as it tickled his sense of the absurd for Claudia Barone to present herself in his office posing as a reporter, he wouldn't have let her run through her spiel if he hadn't wanted to know what she was up to. "I haven't agreed yet," he pointed out.

"Oh, well." She said that tolerantly and crossed her legs, sliding one long, silky thigh over the other. "How can I persuade you?"

Then again, those legs might be the real culprit. The moment she'd appeared in his doorway in her lipstick-red suit he'd wanted to get her into the visitor's chair in front of his desk. He'd wanted to find out how far that one-inch-too-short skirt hiked up.

They were world-class legs, he thought regretfully. And she knew it. She'd crossed and uncrossed them four times since she sat down. "I don't imagine you can."

Not a whit discouraged, she launched into a repetition of her asinine story, her hands flying enthusiastically. It was an intriguing contrast, he thought. Her posture was very proper—shoulders squared, spine straight—and she certainly didn't raise her voice. But her gestures were as loud as the color of her suit.

Even on ten minutes' acquaintance, he could tell Claudia Barone was crammed with contradictions. She looked like the prototype for a tall, cool sip of blond elegance. She was pale and slim—skinny, he told himself—with blue eyes and classic features marred by a nose too assertive for its setting. Her honey-colored hair was pulled back in a kind of a roll at the back, very sleek and polished. The cut of her suit was conservative, too, if you ignored where the hemline hit.

And the color. Which was echoed in the siren-red gloss she'd sleeked over a cute little rosebud mouth.

Her story might be crazy, but her voice was worth listening to, even if it did tug at memories he'd prefer stayed safely buried.

She didn't really look like his ex-wife. Bianca had been a blonde, too, but the color had been courtesy of Clairol, not nature. Not that he knew for a fact

Claudia Barone's sunny shade hadn't come from a bottle, too. There was one sure way to find out.... Don't go there, he told himself, even as his body enthusiastically endorsed the proposed investigation.

But she sure sounded like Bianca. That smoky alto was uncannily familiar, though that had to be sheer coincidence. The Contis and the Barones were no more related than the Hatfields and McCoys had been, and for similar reasons. Her accent was the same as Bianca's, too, but that was no fluke. Upper-class Boston was Miss Claudia Barone's natural habitat.

Unlike the office of a thoroughly working-class detective. Ethan steepled his fingers on the desk and smiled at her blandly. "How can you call the article 'A Day in the Life of a Private Investigator' if you're planning to follow me around for a week?"

"Oh, it will be a composite day." She waved that away. "Not a literal day. That would actually be deceptive, wouldn't it? Any given day might not be typical at all. It's much more accurate to pick and choose parts from several days."

"Then you should call it 'A Typical Day.' Or 'An Average Day.'"

"Perhaps you're right." She turned the wattage up on her smile. "Whatever I call the article, it will be great publicity for your agency. *Free* publicity. And I won't be any bother, truly. What do you say?"

"Free publicity is usually welcome. The only problem I can see is that you aren't a reporter."

She didn't even blink. "What makes you say that?"

Maybe it was her casual attitude toward her own lies that made him decide to do it. Or that perverse sense of humor his uncle had warned him about. Or maybe it was those legs—those mile-long, silk-clad legs she'd been showing off ever since she sat down. "First, there's your shoes."

"My shoes?" She looked down as if checking that the red-leather pumps were still there. "What's wrong with my shoes?"

"Not a thing. Except that no one on a reporter's salary can afford custom-made Italian shoes. The coat looks too expensive, too."

"Well, damn." The mild epithet came out sounding quite ladylike. "I spent three hours shopping for this suit yesterday at a couple of those chain stores that pop up like mushrooms at all the malls. I wanted something with a touch of class, even if it had to be modestly priced to suit the image. Why should being a reporter mean one lacks taste?" She paused expectantly.

"No reason, I suppose," he said, fascinated. She had to be a natural blonde. She *sounded* blond.

"That's what I thought. Stacy wanted me to wear this shapeless pants suit in a dreary shade of brown. Of course," she added with the tone of one wanting to be fair, "*she* can wear earth colors. They turn my complexion muddy. But the style was impossible." She glanced down at her suit with some satisfaction. "I found this on sale for eighty-seven dollars. Can you believe that? But I do so dislike off-the-rack shoes. They always rub or pinch somewhere, especially when they're new. And I didn't think you'd know enough about women's shoes to spot the difference."

''Because I'm not from your background?'' His voice took on an edge.

She rolled her eyes. ''Because you're a *man.* Men never know the least thing about women's clothing, not unless they—'' Now she blinked, startled. ''You aren't, are you? Inclined toward women's clothing yourself, I mean.''

''Good God. No.''

This time her smile crinkled up the corners of her eyes. It looked more natural that way. ''I must say, I'm pleased to hear that. Though I shouldn't be. It's none of my business, but one learns so little if one is overly concerned about that sort of thing, don't you find?''

It was time to get rid of her, before he became too fascinated by the prospect of what absurd thing she'd say next. His uncle had also warned about Ethan's tendency to let his fascination with people distract him. Ethan shoved his chair back and stood. ''You didn't have to pretend to be a reporter, you know.''

''No?'' She watched curiously as he rounded his desk. ''Does that mean you'll let me be part of your investigation?''

When frogs fly. ''It means that a lot of women find P.I.s…appealing.'' He loaded the words with innuendo and let himself enjoy a leisurely visual journey over her body. Small, high breasts…slim waist…smooth hips…and those drool-worthy legs. Pity he had to chase them, and the rest of that enticing package, back out the door. ''Not many are as gorgeous as you are, though.''

With that, he bent and clamped his hands on the

arms of her chair, penning her in. At last her eyes turned wary. "You've misunderstood."

"Don't be embarrassed." He leaned in closer. Her breasts were rising and falling a little too fast beneath the red wool jacket. He turned his smile into a smirk. "I'm flattered. I'm sure we can work out a way to get better acquainted."

Up close, her eyes looked different. The irises were summer-sky blue, but they had a darker ring around the outside that was almost green. His gaze dipped to her red, red lips. She licked them. His heartbeat jacked way up.

Something stabbed down on the arch of his left foot. Hard. He yelped and straightened. Why, that little—! She'd stomped on his foot with the heel of one of those wicked red shoes.

"You should be ashamed of yourself," she said sternly. "Sexual intimidation is not playing nice."

"Playing nice?" He snorted. "What about that thing you kept doing with your legs? And the way you licked your lips just now?"

Guilt flashed across her face, but she tilted her chin up. "That wasn't intimidation."

"No, that's not the word I'd use for it." He propped his hip against his desk, crossed his arms and scowled at her. He'd try plain old intimidation this time. A man his size usually didn't have any trouble pulling that off. "Unless you plan on following through with what you were offering, I'd say it's time for you to leave."

She didn't budge. "I think you knew who I was all along."

"Of course I did. I'm investigating the fire at the

Baronessa plant. I've got a newspaper photo of you in my file."

"But I don't have anything to do with the plant or the company."

"You're a Barone, and I'm a thorough kind of a guy." And she'd had her face in the paper often enough—the society pages, of course.

She leaned forward. The neckline of her suit gapped enough to give him a glimpse of cleavage. "Listen, that fire was— Oh, for heaven's sake." She glanced at where he was looking and straightened. "I know you think of sex seven times a minute or something like that. You can't help it, being a man. But could you please *try* to pay attention? This is important."

"I can pay attention and look down your top at the same time," he assured her. "Being a man, I'm used to that kind of multitasking."

She chuckled. It was low and husky and caught him by surprise. "Your point," she conceded. "But not set and match. *My* point is that you're investigating the weird things that have been happening with Baronessa lately—the tampering with the gelato at the tasting. The arson at the plant. Obviously we need to know who your client is and what you've learned."

"Obviously, I'm not going to tell you."

"You need the cooperation of Baronessa employees. I can get that for you. All I ask in return is a little information. Or the chance to accompany you while you uncover information."

"No. And don't bother to wave a checkbook at me. I don't take bribes."

"Did I suggest that?" She was indignant. "I

wouldn't have gone to all this trouble to trick information out of you if I thought money would work."

His lips twitched. "Just as well. Your brother already tried."

A crease formed in her forehead. "Derrick? He wasn't supposed to. We agreed that I'd handle things. Well." She waved a hand dismissively. "Never mind that. I—"

His phone rang. He picked it up. "Mallory Investigations."

It was Nick Charles, the arson investigator in charge of the Baronessa case—and a good friend of Ethan's cousin, Mel. Nick didn't really have anything for him; mostly he was fishing, himself. Ethan dragged out the conversation, keeping his responses uninformative, just to make his audience squirm with curiosity. Petty, maybe, but a man took what satisfaction he could. Lord knew it was all the satisfaction he was likely to get from Ms. Claudia Nose-in-the-Air Barone.

When he hung up, she had her purse in her lap. "If you'd believed I was a reporter, would you have let me tag along?"

"Probably not. Reporters aren't entitled to the details of my investigation, either."

She sighed. "You're not going to be helpful, are you?"

"Sleep with me and see how helpful I can be." The suggestion slipped out before he could edit it.

"You don't mean that," she informed him, and opened the big clutch-style purse. "Smile." She pulled out a little camera—one of those new digital jobs that aren't much bigger than a wallet.

"What the— Hey!" He held a hand in front of his face a second after the flash went off.

"For my collection," she said breezily, retrieving her coat from the other chair.

No, not a coat, he realized as she slung it on. A cape that fell to mid-calf. Her dramatic side had apparently won out over the proper Boston deb on that particular shopping trip.

Her smile was perfectly polite. "Thank you for your time, Mr. Mallory. When you change your mind about working with me, let me know. I'm sure a thorough man like yourself has my phone number in that file of yours."

He watched the gorgeous legs move briskly out his door and out of his life. She had a damned fine behind, too—high, round and not as skinny as the rest of her.

Not that the rest of her was really skinny. He sighed and reached for his phone. He might lie for a living, but he didn't lie to himself. Ever. Fact was, she was packaged just right. Incredible legs.

Incredible ego, too. Ethan punched in a number he didn't have to look up. Conceited little society twit. Did she really think he was going to invite her to tag along just because she wanted him to? He'd have to be nuts.

The phone was answered on the third ring. "Sal," Ethan said to his client and former father-in-law, Salvatore Conti, head of the family that occupied eight or nine slots on the Barones' Top Ten list of enemies. "You'll never guess who just showed up in my office."

* * *

At eight-thirty that night, Claudia had her hands full of milk—two gallon jugs of it, to be precise. She was in her kitchen. Her best friend since the third grade, Stacy Farquhar, stood near the pantry, watching her suspiciously.

Claudia's kitchen occupied the rear end of her apartment. It was divided from the long, narrow living area by an ivy-covered lattice and the dining table, a glass slab set on a cast-iron frame. Her dining table could seat twelve, and sometimes did. Tonight it held an empty pizza box, two paper plates and a few scattered bits of mushroom and bell pepper.

Claudia was very fond of bell peppers. "Grab the olive oil from the pantry, would you?" she said, using her hip to swing the refrigerator door shut.

"What are you going to do with that milk?" Stacy's voice was filled with accusation. "You said you'd fill me in while we gave ourselves pedicures. Weird ones, maybe, but so much of what you do is weird."

"Don't be silly. What could be more natural than olive oil, salt and milk?" Claudia pulled out a soup pot and poured the milk in a gallon at a time. "You're allergic to so many things, I thought we'd try—"

"I'm allergic to milk!"

"You're allergic to *drinking* it. This is for soaking our feet after we give them the salt-and-olive oil scrub. You've heard of milk baths, for heaven's sake. Now, quit squinting at me and go get us a couple of towels, okay?"

Stacy rolled her eyes and headed for the linen closet. "I don't know why I let you do this to me. It's not as if I've forgotten the time you persuaded me to try out for the boxing team. I still have nightmares.... Hey, the printer's finished.''

She darted into Claudia's bedroom, which was affixed to the rest of the apartment like an afterthought about midway down the living area. And emerged waving the just-printed photo. ''You've been holding out on me.''

''I told you what happened.'' Claudia tested the milk with the tip of her finger. Still cold. She turned the gas up a bit.

''You said Ethan Mallory reminded you of a grizzly bear.'' She slapped the image down on the counter. ''Exhibit A: photograph of major hunk who does not look like any kind of bear.''

Claudia glanced at the photo. Crisp brown hair that would curl if it weren't cut so ruthlessly short. Hazel eyes framed by dark, extravagant lashes, that might have looked pretty if they hadn't been set in such an uncompromisingly masculine face.

''He's very big,'' she offered, trying to remember just why she'd thought of a grizzly bear when she met him.

''He's an ex-football player, you said. From his college days. Of course he's big.''

''Solid, too. And not just physically. I had the feeling it takes a lot to rile him. Not because he lacks a temper, but because he's so insufferably confident that anything other than a direct hit just rolls off. I guess it was the way he loomed over me when he had me pinned in the chair that made me think of a grizzly bear.'' Claudia headed for the pantry for the olive oil. ''Are you going to get us some towels, or not?''

Stacy opened a drawer, grabbed two dish towels and tossed them on the table. ''And just when did he pin you in a chair?''

''I told you he tried to intimidate me.''

''Humph.'' Stacy grabbed a mixing bowl from the cupboard. ''He can't be all that bright. A runaway train wouldn't intimidate you.''

''No, I think he's sharp enough.'' Claudia paused, frowning at the container of salt in her hand. ''Too bright, maybe. And very stubborn. He isn't going to be easy to work with. Oh, well.'' She shrugged and put the salt and olive oil on the table. ''I have to work with what's available, not with what's ideal.''

''Claudia.'' Stacy's tone was ominous now. ''He's smart. He wears his hair short. He's got shoulders like a—well, like a football player. And he's domineering. Is he successful? Leader of the pack in his field?''

''Confident and assertive are *not* synonyms for domineering.'' She went to check the milk. Nice and hot. ''He does wear his hair short, doesn't he?'' Claudia had an image of the surly Mr. Mallory with his hair grown out enough to curl, cherublike, around that hard face. She grinned. ''Curls would interfere with his tough-guy image.''

''Oh, Lord. He's big, sexy, macho as hell. He's practically the archetype. *Your* archetype.''

''I wouldn't say that Ethan Mallory is at the top of his profession. He's made himself a nice little niche in the detective business here in Boston, investigating white-collar crimes, but...'' Claudia decided not to think about that. ''The milk's ready.''

Stacy dragged out a chair, plunked herself down and fixed Claudia with her most repressive stare.

Since Stacy's eyes swallowed about half her face, she looked like a cute, green-eyed owl. The green, of course, was supplied by her contacts. Without them she couldn't have seen who she was glaring at. "You are not to have anything further to do with this man."

"Well, I have to. Besides, I've changed."

"You've made one of your plans, that's all. You decided to change. That doesn't mean you have changed."

"Quit worrying. I'm reformed," Claudia assured her, setting out two plastic tubs for their feet. "On the wagon. I'm dating Neil."

"Four, five dates—big deal. Besides, Neil is not a cure. He's a symptom."

Claudia paused with the pot of steaming milk in her hands, surprised. "I thought you liked Neil."

"Of course I like Neil. He's my type. But I like caution. I *love* caution. You don't."

"The Neils of this world are an acquired taste. I'm acquiring it. I learned to like coffee, didn't I?"

"Yes, but you still don't like spinach."

"I do, too. Sort of."

"It makes you throw up."

Since that observation was hard to dispute—Stacy had been at the restaurant when a serving of pasta Florentine had sent Claudia running for the ladies' room—Claudia ignored it. She poured the milk carefully into each plastic tub. "Now for the exfoliating. Mix a heaping handful of salt with some olive oil."

"I don't know about this." Stacy eyed the ingredients dubiously.

Claudia rolled her eyes. "You don't quibble over spreading that green gunk all over your face, with who knows how many chemicals and preservatives in it, but you're worried about rubbing a little olive oil on your feet?''

''If God had wanted us to put olive oil on our feet, She would already have put it in a lotion sold at Filene's.''

''If you don't trust me, trust my grandmother. She told me about this.''

That worked—as Claudia had known it would. Stacy was nuts about Claudia's Italian grandmother. Of course, it had actually been Claudia's mother's mother, the very proper Bostonian, who'd read about this in some magazine, not her father's thoroughly Italian mother. But mentioning that wouldn't help Stacy relax and enjoy herself.

The two of them rubbed their feet with gritty oil. ''So do you think your plan will work?'' Stacy asked. ''The one to make Ethan Mallory let you tag along on the investigation, I mean. Not your other plan, with Neil. That's doomed.''

''Not right away.'' Claudia gave her heel a little extra attention. Calluses built up there so quickly. ''He's stubborn, like I said. He'll try to wiggle or trick his way out.''

Right after her meeting with the detective, Claudia had e-mailed the photograph she'd taken of him to her cousin Nicholas, COO of Baronessa. He, in turn, had sent it to all Baronessa department heads and supervisors, telling them that no one, but no one, was to speak with Ethan Mallory or allow him onto corporate property unless he was accompanied by a Barone family member.

That family member, of course, being Claudia.

They'd settled that at the family council two nights ago. She had the time and the energy to devote to this complication. The others didn't. Besides, she was good at fixing things. And boy, did things need fixing right now.

"So what's plan B? I know you have a plan B. You always do."

"I'll just follow him around, see what he's up to, that sort of thing. *That* will annoy him." Claudia eased her feet into the warm milk and wiggled her toes. "But I think I'll enjoy it. I've never done detective work before."

"You're getting carried away here, Nancy Drew. You're supposed to find out who this guy's client is, not start playing detective yourself."

"My family is counting on me."

"They don't expect you to turn into Nancy Drew."

"Things are wrong. More wrong than I'd realized."

"Of course there's something wrong. Like arson, for one. Good Lord, your sister was nearly killed. Has she remembered anything else?"

"Nothing about the night of the fire. And of course arson is wrong, but..." The unease she felt went deeper than any anxiety about the family corporation. She pulled out one foot and began drying it.

Claudia was happy that Baronessa existed, both for the opportunities it provided several family members and the wealth it generated. She wouldn't be able to accomplish nearly so much if she were tied to a nine-to-five job. But the core of her unease lay in the fallout from the sabotage—fault lines within her family she hadn't known existed, and still hadn't identified clearly.

Her sister had survived the bout with amnesia and met a delicious man while recovering; Emily should be head-over-heels happy. Mostly she was, but something was eating at her, something from the night of the fire that she couldn't remember. Then there was Derrick.

Claudia sighed. Sometimes she thought her brother was a changeling. In a family of overachievers, he consistently…missed. Not by much. His failures, like everything else about him, were unremarkable, more likely to irritate than command attention. Poor Derrick. He did try. Lately, though, his muddled efforts to push to the head of the line seemed to have acquired an edge.

Then there was her cousin Maria, who had turned weird overnight, running off to who-knew-where. Uncle Carlo and Aunt Moira were worried. That was so not like Maria.

Stacy broke into her brooding. "You can't fix everything, 'Dia."

Claudia's chin came up. "I can try."

A muffled ringing announced a phone call. Claudia muttered at herself as she conducted a quick hunt. She managed herself quite as ruthlessly as she did everyone else, and did not understand why this one quirk of hers refused to vanish on command. The phone was *never* where it was supposed to be.

This time it turned out to be in the pantry. "Hello?"

"Cute trick with the photo. I've decided to accept your deal."

The voice wasn't one she could forget. Not this quickly. Not when it set up such a delicious resonance inside her. "I hadn't expected to hear from you this soon."

"It seemed better to call and capitulate than to pout and drag things out. I have to be able to speak with Baronessa personnel to complete my investigation."

"I see. A commendable attitude. Ah, I do want to make sure we're talking about the same deal. This is not about me sleeping with you, correct?"

Stacy's eyes went barn-owl wide.

"That's no longer a requirement."

"Good. About your client—"

"That's not part of the deal, either."

"How shall we begin our collaboration, then?"

"I'll pick you up at nine tomorrow morning."

"All right. I'll be waiting downstairs—the parking is impossible here. I assume you have my address in that file of yours?"

He chuckled, agreed that he did, and told her to look for a nondescript gray Buick.

A dangerous man, Claudia thought as she disconnected. That deep, rumbly chuckle had vibrated right out of the phone and into her belly. She tapped the phone with one finger. "That was too easy. He turned belly-up in less than six hours."

"So? You got what you wanted. Not that I'm surprised. Or are you disappointed that he wasn't more of a challenge?"

"Of course not. I don't want him to be difficult to handle. That would be counterproductive." Claudia put the phone down, a frown tucking a small vee between her brows. She *had* gotten what she wanted.

So where was the slick, greasy feel in her stomach coming from?

The pizza, obviously. And maybe she was a teensy bit worried about what Ethan Mallory might be cooking up…and how she'd react the next time she saw him. She sighed. "I think the challenge is still to come."

Two

At nine o'clock the next morning, Claudia stood in front of her apartment building reading a grant application and making notes in the margins. Her fingers were freezing, but she hated fumbling with the pages through gloves. The rest of her was comfortable enough, though she did hope Mallory wouldn't keep her waiting long.

She'd been up since six, but that was nothing unusual. She always got up at six. Claudia believed in the discipline of routine. Yoga first, then yogurt, cereal and coffee followed by her shower. She'd dressed, dried her hair, applied makeup, placed a sell order with her broker, answered e-mail and spoken with the manager of a women's center.

The only chore that had presented a problem was dressing. What did one wear to go detecting?

She'd spent ten minutes trapped by indecision, pulling out one thing after another. Claudia hated indecision even more than she hated being dressed inappropriately, so in the end she'd opted for casual. Black blended in almost anywhere. Of course, her electric-blue leather coat didn't exactly blend in, but unrelieved black was so boring. She'd pulled on her oldest pair of boots in case they went tramping around the burned-out plant.

The problem was, they might be going anywhere. She hadn't asked. Claudia tapped her pen against her bottom lip, irritated. She'd allowed herself to be distracted by Ethan Mallory's low, rumbly voice. Or possibly his chuckle. Or the memory of his shoulders.

A horn honked. Claudia woke from her reverie to see a dirty, gunmetal-gray, four-door sedan stopped in the traffic lane. She stuffed the grant proposal into her satchel and darted between the parked cars.

Mallory leaned across the bench seat to open the door for her and she slid in, her arrival trumpeted by the horn of the driver behind the Buick. Some people had no patience.

"Good morning," she said brightly, eyeing his tie with fascination. It was blue with green squiggles and didn't go with his suit, which was the same color as his car, but cleaner. About the best thing that could be said for the tailoring was that it had the proper number of sleeves and trouser legs. He'd tossed a khaki trench coat in the back seat that would look perfectly ghastly with the gray suit. "Where are we going first?"

"Huntington Avenue." He accelerated smoothly.

"Baronessa headquarters, in other words."

"Yep."

Her heartbeat had no business speeding up. And her tummy was going to have to get over that lurch of anticipatory joy, because nothing was going to happen.

What was it with her, anyway? He wasn't even good-looking—not the way Drake had been, at least. Or Charles, for that matter. His hair was a nondescript brown, his lips were too thin and his nose was crooked. Aside from the to-die-for body, he looked quite ordinary.

Ordinary, that is, for a tough guy. She'd bet he developed five o'clock shadow by 4:00 p.m. But his eyes didn't fit the image. The irises were a cool dun color speckled with green that, at a distance, blended into hazel. Speckled eyes, set off by lashes too dark and long for either his hair or his gender. And...and she was staring, blast her, and he was smiling, blast him, an irritating little quirk of those thin lips announcing that he'd noticed her attention.

Claudia switched to a safer visual inquiry—the debris on the seat, the back seat and the floorboard. Her eyebrows lifted.

He noticed that, too. "I use my car as a rolling office sometimes. Things accumulate."

"I see. No, I don't. That would explain the files, books and calculator. Possibly the newspaper, candy wrappers and empty soda cans, too, if we allow for a degree of slobbiness. But not the Slinky, the Rubik's Cube or the empty mayonnaise jar."

"Those are for stakeouts. They can get pretty boring."

Okay, so the toys were just toys. She wouldn't ask about the handcuffs. "What do you do with the jar?"

"You don't want to know."

"I wouldn't have asked if I didn't."

He flashed her a grin. "Emergency urinal."

Oh. It didn't *look* used.... Hastily she mentioned traffic. Traffic was the Boston equivalent of talking about the weather. Often it segued into a discussion of the Big Dig. Would the underground highway ever be finished? Was it an enormous boondoggle or an engineering feat to rival the Great Pyramids?

"Traffic sucks," he said. "Why were you the appointed family member to deal with me? You aren't connected to Baronessa, except by dividend checks. Seems like someone like, say, your cousin the corporate president would swing a bigger stick."

"I believe the size of my stick was sufficient to get me into your car this morning. Who do you want to see at headquarters? My cousin the corporate president?"

"Him, yes. Also your cousin, Gina."

"Why?"

"I'm looking into the tampering that occurred last Valentine's Day, too. It was almost certainly the same person. Gina ran that show. I'll need to talk to your brother Derrick, as well."

"Why Derrick?"

He gave her a sardonic look. "He's in charge of quality control. Seems like having your new flavor tampered with was a pretty major failure in his department. And his office was at the plant, before it burned."

Yes, it was. He'd complained about that often

enough. Derrick was ever watchful for a slight, worried that his cousins were achieving more than him, getting more perks, more recognition.

Claudia chewed on her lip. Derrick had been especially difficult ever since the fiasco at the gala held to promote the newest Baronessa flavor—which had now been scrapped. Someone had adulterated the passion fruit gelato with habanero pepper juice. If that hadn't been bad enough, one of the guests had suffered an allergic reaction and had to be rushed to the hospital. Derrick seemed to think the whole thing was a personal attack on his effectiveness.

''You can get me in to speak with these people, right?''

''Oh, sure.'' She flapped a hand in a vague affirmative. The traffic was living up to his pithy description, creeping along at a snail's pace. At this rate she'd be trapped in this car with him for another twenty minutes. Claudia resolved not to look at him too often. ''You have any ideas about the culprit yet?''

''Yeah.'' He slid her a look out of those sneaky, two-toned eyes. ''It's someone who's real unhappy with you Barones.''

Claudia unbuttoned her coat, wondering again who had hired this man. ''You think it's personal, rather than a business competitor who has lost his sense of proportion?''

''I'm not ruling out the possibility of a competitor. There's Snowcream, Inc. And there's Anderson Enterprises. Baronessa has taken over several of their markets in the last two years.''

Uh-oh. Did he know about Drake? She studied him

warily. Yes. Too much of a coincidence for him to mention Anderson otherwise. Of course, he couldn't know *everything.* Just the more public portions of what had turned out to be an all-too-public romantic debacle.

"Anderson sells a good deal more than ice cream, Mr. Mallory. Baronessa only sells gelato. We might irritate them, but we only compete with one corner of their business. Arson isn't a reasonable response to a small dip in the profit column."

"Business rivalries can escalate beyond the reasonable when there's a personal element involved. And from what I hear, you and the Anderson son and heir were involved very personally." He shook his head. "No accounting for taste, I guess, but just what did you see in that pin-striped piranha? Aside from the teeth and great suits, that is."

It sounded as if he'd met Drake. Emotions rose like a swarm of gnats, putting a tug on Claudia's lips that was part annoyance, part amusement. If worse came to worst, she wouldn't have to fight her way past any illusions created by Ethan Mallory's sartorial brilliance, would she? Maybe she could actually have the quick, hot affair her body was urging....

Bad idea. Really bad. "Tell me, do you actually *have* a client? Someone who's hired you, that is. It occurred to me you might be doing a favor for an old friend."

He lifted one eyebrow. They were very nice eyebrows, darker than his hair, like his eyelashes, and with a pleasant arch. Expressive eyebrows for such a tough face. "So you know about Bianca and me."

"Well, of course. Though Bianca took her maiden

name back after the divorce, so I didn't place your name right away. It's been a few years, hasn't it? Not that I mistake gossip—'' she fluttered a hand as if fanning away the chaff ''—for reality. Was your parting amicable?''

''Now, why would you think that was any of your business?''

''I'd like to determine where your biases lie. And your loyalties. I could easily imagine that Sal Conti played some part in the breakup of your marriage, for example, leaving you with the burning desire to embarrass or hurt him in return. But you might have remained fond of your ex, and be determined to clear her family.''

''You go right ahead and speculate, honey. I know how fascinated some women are by other people's love lives.''

''Well, *honey,* while I'm enjoying my speculations, you can circle the block. You just passed the Baronessa building.''

Ethan didn't actually have to circle the block, since the parking garage that served the building had an entrance on the nearest cross street. Claudia directed him to the portion reserved for visitors. She didn't say a word about his having almost passed his target. She didn't have to. Her smirk said it all.

As soon as he cut the engine, she jumped out. That didn't surprise him. This wasn't a woman to sit around waiting on a man, or anyone or anything else. He bet she'd skipped learning to walk in favor of hitting the ground running, and hadn't stopped since.

He hit the button that locked his car. She was

standing on the other side, tapping one foot impatiently, her hands thrust in the pockets of that absurdly bright coat that looked like a double dip of sky.

"So tell me," he said companionably, "is it true you dumped a whole carton of melted ice cream on Drake Anderson's head in front of the power-suit crowd at the Radius?"

She flicked him an annoyed glance. "It was only *slightly* melted."

"Pretty stupid of him to have shot off his mouth that way, where you could overhear him."

"Drake has a problem knowing when to keep his mouth shut. It's a common failing." The disdain in her glance suggested it was one Ethan shared. She turned and set off briskly for the door to the lobby.

Damn, but she was cute. Ethan grinned and whistled the first two bars of the *William Tell Overture* as he stretched his legs to catch up with his pretty blond passport.

She held the door open for him. "You haven't talked to anyone here yet, right?" she asked.

"Not yet. I focused on the plant first." And had found one thread worth tugging on, which had led him to headquarters. "I did try to speak to some people here yesterday. Got turned away." He lifted his eyebrow. "Good block."

"I do what I can."

The building itself was one of those oversize glass-and-chrome splinters modern architects were fond of, buffed and buttressed by steel. Attractive enough, Ethan supposed, in its way. But he preferred brick or stone. The foyer made him think of bank lobbies—lots of glass, a gleaming tile floor, with potted plants huddled in the corners trying valiantly to soften things. One wall held the bank of elevators; another was dedicated to a photographic history of Baronessa's early years.

The executive offices occupied the fifth floor. He pushed the up button.

She pulled off her coat and draped it over her arm. Ethan sighed with pleasure. Nothing like a long, cool blonde dressed all in black. She'd left her hair down today, too, which made up for the fact that she wasn't wearing a skimpy little skirt like yesterday's. He planned to enjoy looking at her while he could. She wouldn't be around long.

"Who are we talking to first?" she asked. "Nicholas?"

"Good question. I need to see a personnel file. How do I obtain it?"

"First you tell me whose file you need, and why."

He leaned against the wall and crossed his arms. "And if I do, can you get the file for me?"

Her lips pursed. "I think so, but I have to know why I'm getting it first."

"Ed Norblusky. He worked at the plant until three days after the tasting was sabotaged. He was fired for showing up for work drunk. Seems he shot his mouth off afterward about how he'd teach 'those rich bastards' a thing or two. And he's disappeared."

She bounced on the balls of her feet, excited. "You said you didn't know who it was! This Norblusky—"

"May have just moved, not intentionally disappeared. And people blow off steam all the time without setting fire to an ice cream plant to make their point. But he's worth checking into. I need the name and address of his last employer, his next of kin, his social security number—all of which should be in his personnel file.''

She nodded decisively. ''I can get it. Nicholas and I deal well together. That's whose approval we'll need.''

''Tell me what he's like.''

''A man with a mission,'' she said as the elevator doors opened. Three people got out, giving them curious glances. ''He always has a plan, a goal to shoot for. When he was eight, his mission was a puppy.''

''Did he get it?''

''Of course. A hyperactive little Dalmatian, cute as could be. He took care of it, too, right from the first. That's why his missions usually succeed. He plans, he works toward that plan and he follows through.''

''What's his mission these days?''

''Being the world's best daddy, I think.'' Her smile was wide and bright, but he noticed that it didn't push any crinkles into the corners of her eyes. ''Or maybe Husband of the Year. I'm sure perfect Chief Operations Officer is still high on the list, too.''

''Do you always do that?''

''What?''

''Smile harder when something hurts.''

Her eyebrows twitched crossly. ''I don't know *what* you're talking about. I'm very fond of Nicholas. Naturally, I'm happy for him.''

''If all it took to make us happy was the happiness of someone we cared about, the world would need only one happy person. Chain reaction, you see. The original happy person would make everyone he or she met happy, and they'd make all their friends and family happy, and they—''

''You have a strange mind, you know that?''

''So I've been told. Did you know that your eyes only crinkle up at the corners when you really mean your smiles?''

She blinked, opened her mouth, then closed it again.

''I guess not.'' How about that. She was speechless. He bet that didn't happen often. Whistling softly, he straightened and punched the button for the fifth floor.

For some reason Claudia's stomach was tight. Not because Ethan Mallory's observation had upset her, of course. He was way off base. She was happy for Nicholas, who deserved every drop of his recent good fortune.

No, it was her distressingly competitive nature that was to blame. Claudia had long ago acknowledged that she just plain liked to win. The score between her and Mallory wasn't quite even—she remained one up due to her flanking maneuver with the photograph—but he'd certainly narrowed her lead.

He was an annoyingly observant man, though. That was a good quality in a detective, she conceded privately as the elevator carried them to the fifth floor. But tricky in an opponent.

Fortunately, Nicholas wasn't in a meeting or otherwise unavailable. Claudia had very little time to chat with his assistant before they were told to go on in, which was probably just as well. Mrs. Peabody was trying to give away puppies.

Claudia liked Nicholas's office. The window-walls made it sunny when the weather was clear, and even on a gray November morning like this they imparted a spacious feeling. Nicholas was seated when they entered, a big, dark-haired man with what Claudia liked to call laser eyes—sharp and keen as a scalpel.

At the moment he was looking decidedly wary. He stood and walked around his desk, holding out his hands. "I'm delighted to see you, of course, but…you haven't decided Baronessa needs your attention, have you?"

She chuckled as she took his hands, leaning in to kiss him on the cheek. "Don't worry. You've done too good a job here. There's nothing for me to fix. Aside from the problems we discussed the other night, that is. Nicholas, this is Ethan Mallory."

"Ah. The detective." Nicholas nodded, but she noticed he held on to her hands long enough to make it unnecessary to shake Ethan's. "Mr. Mallory. You're here with questions, I assume."

"That, and a request." He slanted Claudia an amused glance. "Properly vetted by the family's tame dragon, here."

Nicholas smiled. "Don't bet on the 'tame' part."

Claudia had no objection to being called a dragon. They were beautiful, powerful beasts, after all, highly intelligent and, in Chinese folklore, the repositories of wisdom. But she didn't care for *tame*. "I am civilized, I trust, but *tame* implies a certain subordination. While I'm perfectly capable of working *with* others—"

"Ha," Nicholas muttered.

"I'll admit I have trouble working *for* others. Shall

we sit down to discuss Ethan's request, or are you on a tight schedule this morning, Nicholas?''

Nicholas waved at the visitors' chairs. ''By all means, sit down. I can give you a few minutes.''

They all found their places—Nicholas behind his desk, Claudia and Ethan in the cushy chairs opposite. Nicholas tented his hands on his desk. ''So, what is this request?''

''Two requests, actually,'' Ethan said. ''First, I need to talk to a few of your people about how the tasting was arranged. Claudia assures me she can get me in to see them, but I figured I should clear it with you, too. Maybe you can answer some of my questions. You must have ordered an internal investigation.''

Nicholas met her eyes for a moment. She knew what he was thinking—Derrick would be furious if his competence was questioned. Especially by Nicholas. ''We did perform an internal investigation. My time's a little short this morning. It would be faster for you to read a copy of the report.'' He buzzed Mrs. Peabody and told her to pull it and make a copy. ''If you still have questions after reading that,'' he said to Ethan, ''you may speak to anyone Claudia approves. I trust her judgment.''

Ethan's fingers tapped once on the arm of the chair. ''Thanks. I also need to see the personnel file on a former employee—Ed Norblusky.''

''Norblusky,'' Nicholas repeated thoughtfully. ''Why?''

Ethan repeated what he'd told Claudia about Ed Norblusky. Claudia listened with half an ear, willing to let him make his own case and intervene only as needed.

She should have told him it was no business of his how she smiled. Good grief, most people had a whole wardrobe of smiles—grins, grimaces, openmouthed laughter, polite smiles, wry little twitches. Crinkly eyes probably caused wrinkles, anyway.

She certainly wasn't so petty as to begrudge her cousin his good fortune. Nicholas been through a rough time, first with the girlfriend from hell, then learning—two years after the fact—that he was a father. He deserved the happiness he'd found with Gail.

And their couple-ness did *not* make her feel left out. Not really. Maybe there was a twinge of discomfort now and then. Just because one was strong didn't mean one wanted to be strong every minute, or alone every night…but she'd learned her lesson. When a woman of twenty-eight couldn't sustain a relationship past the four-month mark, it was obvious she had a serious flaw.

Claudia believed in facing her own deficits straightforwardly. After her last romantic disaster—the one with Drake—she'd done quite a bit of soul-searching. In the end, there had been only one possible conclusion: her sexual antennae were tuned to the wrong channel.

Strong, take-charge men revved Claudia's motor. Men who ran businesses or rose to the top of their chosen fields, deliciously *male* beings who could match her wit for wit, strength for strength.

Men who didn't want her back.

It had come as a shock when she finally accepted that the kind of men she was attracted to were in turn attracted to female pillows—soft women, squishy and delicate. Women who, by contrast, made their men feel even more hard and strong and male. Exceptions did exist, but were so rare as to be statistically negligible. Look at Tony's new wife, or either of Max's wives—the one he'd been rebounding from when he and Claudia were together, or the one he married a month after they broke up. Then there was that bit of fluff Hal had been sleeping with on the side…no, she couldn't count that. Hal belonged outside her test sample. Infidelity was the symptom of a weak character, not a strong one.

After Hal had come Drake. She'd been in recovery from that humiliation when she'd finally woken up and smelled the testosterone. *All* of Drake's other romantic liaisons had been Pillow Women. Every one except her. That should have warned her, but she hadn't wanted to see the truth until she'd overheard him at a party.

He'd been planning to dump her. He'd laughed at her with his friend, and said horrible, humiliating things about her lack of femininity, her—well, never mind. She'd been particularly foolish about Drake, but she'd learned her lesson.

The men she wanted sometimes did want her back, but they got over it. This made for a pretty good-sized flaw, but she had a plan. She—

"Claudia?" Nicholas waved a hand back and forth. "Where did you go?"

"Oh. Sorry." Frantically she cast her mind back over the last minute or so and grabbed a wisp of memory before it evaporated. "Respecting an employee's privacy is all very well, Nicholas, but this is a criminal investigation.''

''Yes, but Mr. Mallory is not the police. As I just pointed out.''

Whoops. She'd missed that.

Ethan was leaning back in his chair, his legs outstretched, as at ease as if they were talking about football. Or traffic. It was not the reaction most men had to Nicholas. They were such muscular legs, too.... *Behave,* she told herself firmly.

''I can give you my word,'' Ethan said, ''that nothing I learn from a personnel file will be used unless it bears directly on the crimes I'm investigating.''

Damn that deep, rumbly voice of his. It seemed to vibrate things inside of her. ''That seems reasonable, Nicholas.''

His brows twitched up. ''Trust him, do you?''

''Oh, no. I'm sure he's a good liar. He would have to be, in his profession, wouldn't he? But what earthly use could he make of Ed Norblusky's employment history outside of this investigation? I don't think we need to worry about him selling the man's phone number to a telemarketer.''

''No telemarketers,'' Ethan said dryly, ''I promise.''

Nicholas shook his head, but said, ''All right. You can look, Mallory. Claudia, you go with him and make sure he doesn't slip anything into his pocket. And I want to know what you learn when you find this man.''

''I'll keep you posted,'' she assured him.

''If I find any evidence,'' Ethan said, ''it will go to the police. They'll keep you informed, I imagine.''

Nicholas's smile was a masterpiece of cool skepticism. ''No doubt.'' He leaned forward to punch in a number on his speakerphone and asked someone to pull the file on Ed Norblusky. ''My cousin Claudia will be down in a few minutes with a man named Ethan Mallory. They may look at the file, but it's not to leave your office.'' He disconnected. ''Satisfied?''

Ethan nodded. ''Thanks again.'' He stood. ''You recognized Norblusky's name. Mind telling me why?''

''You'll find out soon enough. Norblusky drove the truck that transported the gelato that was tampered with.''

''Nicholas!'' Claudia bounced to her feet. ''Why didn't you say so earlier?''

''I wanted to know Mr. Mallory's reasons for looking for the man.'' He stood. ''Good to meet you, Mr. Mallory.'' This time, he offered his hand.

Claudia wondered what mysterious male test Ethan had passed to rate the handshake. ''I'll see you soon, I'm sure. Tell Gail hello, and give Molly a big, sloppy kiss for me.''

''Will do. I'd like a word with you before you leave.'' He glanced at Ethan. ''Family matters. If you wouldn't mind waiting outside—?''

''No problem.'' Ethan's smile was wide, almost sleepy.

He didn't look like a shark, but Claudia's antennae were quivering. ''You can talk to Mrs. Peabody. Nicholas's assistant? She's very nice.'' And she really needed a home for those puppies.

He gave her a wry look. ''Think I'll read the report

instead. I don't need a puppy.'' With a last nod at Nicholas, he headed for the door.

Claudia frowned at him. He'd seen right through her. How annoying.

As soon as the door closed behind Ethan, Nicholas turned those laser eyes on her, trying to slice through to the back of her head. ''I don't like the look in his eyes when he's watching you.''

''Really?'' Surprised pleasure hummed in her middle. She ignored that. Involuntary responses didn't count. ''I hadn't noticed that kind of look on his face.''

''He doesn't do it when you can see. Claudia.'' He shook his head. ''Mallory intends to trick you.''

''Oh, I know that.'' She waved it aside. ''He doesn't know me very well.''

Nicholas's lips twitched once before he smoothed them out. ''Are you sure you know what you're doing?''

She smiled brightly, easily, at him and tried to make her eyes crinkle. ''Of course. Don't I always?''

Three

By the time Ethan left the building, he was feeling quite satisfied with the bargain he'd struck with his tame dragon. Norblusky's personnel file had been all he'd hoped it would be—references, social security number, the works. Derrick Barone had played least-in-sight, but Gina Barone Kingman had been helpful.

And the report Nicholas had given Ethan was extremely interesting.

Whoever had handled the in-house investigation had done a good job of reconstructing events. The report concluded that the gelato had been adulterated when a person or persons unknown had entered the back of the refrigerated truck ferrying the gelato to the tasting while the truck was stuck in traffic.

Nothing amazing about a truck getting caught in traffic, but Ethan's curiosity was snagged by the reason for that particular traffic jam. A produce truck had spilled bushels of habanero peppers all over the street.

Life was full of bizarre coincidences, and that was probably all this was. But he thought he'd check out the driver of the produce truck, anyway.

Ethan glanced at the woman beside him. Claudia had been elated by the news of Norblusky's connection, then irritated when they learned her brother was gone—to a luncheon appointment, according to his secretary. Two hours before noon. Ethan was definitely curious about Derrick Barone.

It didn't take a body-language genius to interpret the way Claudia tensed up every time Derrick's name was mentioned. Ethan figured that Derrick was the Barones' problem child. Most families had one. That by itself wouldn't make him suspicious, but the report Nicholas had given him had confirmed what Ethan had suspected: the gelato tampering had been an inside job.

The people with the most knowledge and best access to the gelato were all Barones. Admittedly, an employee made a more likely saboteur than someone who was getting rich off Baronessa, but the Barone problem child had expensive tastes. Offered a big-enough bribe from one of Baronessa's competitors, he might have chosen money now over money later.

All of which meant Ethan had to ditch the blonde. Pity, but given half a chance, Ms. Claudia Barone would put herself in charge of his investigation—and she wasn't likely to investigate her brother.

Bossy woman. He smiled, thinking of the way she'd primmed up when he'd referred to her as a *tame* dragon.

"What's that about?" she asked, all blue-eyed suspicion.

"What?" He opened the passenger door for her.

"That sneaky smile. Most of us *do* have different smiles, you know, for different occasions."

"That stung, did it?" He went around to his side, climbed in and tossed the red-bound report in the box in the back seat that held his working files. "I wouldn't worry about it," he told her reassuringly. "I doubt most people notice the difference. Personally, though, I kind of like the crinkles."

"I don't recall expressing an interest in your opinion. My goodness, this car is chilly. Would you turn on the heat, please?"

I shouldn't, he thought as he turned to look at her. *She didn't mean it that way...*but she was so pretty and prissy, and he wouldn't have another chance.

What the hell. He grinned. "Anything you say, Ms. Barone." He seized her face in both hands and planted one on that cupid's bow mouth.

He expected a slap, or even a punch in his stomach. Instead, she went stiff with outrage, like a cat dropped in water.

That, too, was somehow irresistible. Beckoning. He painted a teasing line across her lips with his tongue. Soft lips, so much softer than he'd anticipated...her taste intrigued, beguiled. He forgot why he'd started this, intent on coaxing more from her. His fingers loosened their grip to stroke lightly along both sides of her face, up and down, brailling the part of her that was at once public and intimate.

Her breath caught in a confused little hiccup. Then she did a terrible thing. She opened her mouth to him and fisted her hands in his shirt, kissing him like a shipwreck victim scooped up ragged and starving, with him her first meal.

Lust exploded, wiping his internal landscape clear of thought. The skin was taut and smooth on her cheeks, dangerously soft along her throat. He licked it. Her sweater was a nuisance, but instinct worked fine. He didn't need to think. He sent a hand sliding up under the thick wool, touched skin even softer than on her throat.

She jolted, jerking back. Shocked blue eyes stared at him.

Had he lost his ever-loving mind?

"That was— I didn't mean to—" Ethan exhaled gustily. "A mistake. That was a mistake."

She nodded quickly three times. "Absolutely. Yes. We'll put it out of our minds. It never happened."

"What didn't happen?" His hands had stopped shaking. Good. He reached for the seat belt.

"Ah…exactly." The lips still damp from his twitched. Maybe that was amusement, or maybe she was still short-circuited, too. She fastened her own seat belt as he reversed out of the parking slot. "Where do we go next?"

His body immediately suggested a possible destination and some intriguing side trips. "Gas station," he said hastily.

"Pardon?"

"I need to gas up." And get away from her. Fast.

"Okay, once you've refueled, then what? We have the names of Norblusky's references now. One of them may know where he is."

He nodded. With her natural bent toward taking

charge, that was all that was needed. She was off and running, planning his next few days for him. Which left him free to spin in dizzy dismay.

He knew better. Dammit, he ought to. Claudia Barone was from another world, not the one he knew. That put her off limits. Period.

Some people bounced back fast from a divorce, or so it seemed to Ethan. Not him. The raw-gut flavor of failure had clung to him for years.

He'd had his angry period. Ethan wasn't proud of the way he'd behaved right after Bianca dumped him, but it hadn't lasted long. The lessons he'd learned about anger went too deep for him to stay mad all the time. One morning he'd woken with a woman whose name he didn't know cuddled up to him, her face all shiny and hopeful.

Self-disgust had put a stop to that kind of thing. He'd buried himself in work for a while, and that had been a pretty good way of handling things. He'd made something of himself and the firm; eventually he'd bought out his uncle, and now his only partner was the bank.

After his workaholic years he'd had a fling with self-improvement. There had to have been something wrong with him if his wife couldn't handle more than ten months of his company.

Well, nothing wrong with wanting to fix things when there was a problem, he mused as he headed east on Boylston. But he'd made a major mistake. He'd listened to his female cousins.

They'd insisted women wanted gentle, sensitive men. He'd figured he was okay with the gentle part; after all, a man his size had to be careful with the softer half of the human race. So he'd thought his problem must be the sensitivity deal. Not much doubt he was lacking there. Every woman he knew assured him of that.

Problem was, "sensitive" turned out to be some sort of female code. They all seemed to know what it meant, but none of them could explain it. When he'd asked three of his cousins for specific actions he could take to be sensitive, they'd looked at him funny and shaken their heads. Amy had told him to get in touch with his feelings; Jo had talked about communication and subtext and nonverbal cues. Katherine had just patted his shoulder and said something about lost causes.

The only useful data he'd gotten out of them had been remembering birthdays—there were rules for that, it turned out—washing dishes at least half the time, and never looking at another woman.

Ethan snorted. Birthdays and dishes, yeah, he could handle those. But not to even *look?*

"You don't agree?" Claudia lifted her eyebrows.

He had no idea what she'd just said. "I was thinking," he told her, making a turn. Joe's service station was three blocks up, on the corner. "Probably be good to know if Norblusky had access to the gelato that was used at the tasting. He's no rocket scientist. If he didn't have ready access, he's not a good suspect."

"I see what you mean. Frank Parengeter at the plant would know, wouldn't he? So I guess that's our next stop." She gave her boots an approving glance.

"Mmm. Might be best to let the cops look for Norblusky. They've got a lot more men and resources."

"Then why do people hire you?" she demanded. "If all you're going to do is turn things over to the police, what does anyone need you for?"

"Brains and discretion." He'd found out about Norblusky, not the cops, dammit. "You're just pi—ah, irritated because you wanted to play detective."

She was quiet a moment, and when she spoke it came out more slowly than usual. "You're doing this for money, maybe for professional pride. Those are good reasons, but this is my *family* that's in trouble. I want this person, whoever it is, stopped. I don't want any more incidents. My sister Emily was nearly killed in the last one."

He grimaced. Hadn't he known she'd be complicated? She was supposed to get huffy. Instead, she turned sincere on him.

It didn't make any difference, he assured himself as he turned into the Texaco station on the corner. Sincere amateurs were just as likely to get themselves and him into trouble as the ones who'd watched too many *Magnum, P.I.* reruns. He pulled up at the pump and cut the ignition. "I'll go pay," he said, opening his door. "I could use a can of tonic. You?"

"Not before lunch, thank you."

"Maybe you could pump the gas while I'm at it. You do know how to pump gas?"

"Yes. I bathe myself, too. I've even been known to dial the phone without breaking a nail."

Their eyes met. A smile tugged on his mouth. "You implying I'm stereotyping you?"

"Rich, blond and female does not equal helpless."

The smile widened into a grin. "Ever change your own oil?"

‘‘Don’t get carried away,’’ she advised him, opening her door and sliding out.

Joe was sitting behind the counter, leafing through a magazine. He looked up in disapproval when Ethan walked in. ‘‘Looks like a nice young woman. I thought you’d outgrown this kind of behavior.’’

‘‘I’m not dumping her,’’ Ethan said, exasperated. ‘‘I explained all this. I’m escaping, but it’s purely business.’’

‘‘Pretty thing, too. Long legs, long blond hair…’’ He sighed. ‘‘Real pretty. Doesn’t look like a criminal to me.’’

‘‘She’s not a criminal. She’s a nuisance.’’ Ethan pulled out his wallet.

‘‘You always think your women are a nuisance after a while.’’

‘‘She’s not my woman. Here.’’ He put a twenty on the counter, glancing out the window. He needed to get away before Claudia finished. How long would it take her to realize he wasn’t coming back to the car? ‘‘For the gas. Your car is around back?’’

‘‘If Cindy finds out I helped you trick your girlfriend—’’

‘‘Read my lips. She is not my girlfriend.’’

‘‘Maybe *you* don’t think so. She might, though.’’ Joe glanced out the window again. Claudia was wiping down the windshield with the squeegee. When she stretched, her sweater rode up, giving them a lovely view of her pretty little bottom. ‘‘She’s blond.’’

‘‘I don’t date every blonde who stumbles across my path. The keys, Joe? Or are you backing out on our deal?’’

‘‘No reason you can’t take the T.’’

"Public transportation is fine if it goes everywhere I want to. It doesn't. And you agreed, dammit."

Joe looked stubborn. "I wasn't thinking straight. If you use my car, Cindy will want to know why."

Cindy was Joe's wife, and Ethan's cousin. One of his cousins. His parents had both come from families who had taken the "go forth and multiply" injunction to heart, though they'd had only a single child themselves. Him. "Tell Cindy I borrowed your car because of a case I'm working on. That has the advantage of being true. She won't know about Claudia unless you mention her."

Ethan ought to be feeling pleased. This was a neat trick, worthy of the woman who'd sneaked his photograph yesterday. He felt like pond scum. The kind of slippery slime that coats stagnant water, maybe mixed with a little industrial waste.

That was what he got for kissing her, dammit. Guilt.

"They pull it out of your head," Joe said glumly. "Whatever you don't want them to know, they pull it right out. I don't know how women do that, but they do."

Ethan sighed. Then he snatched the magazine from Joe's hands.

"Hey!"

"Hmm." He glanced at the contents briefly before handing it back. "Hope you're wrong about female telepathy, Joe. If Cindy pulls anything out of your head about Claudia, you'd better be ready for her to read my mind, too. Miss April is pretty memorable. She's likely to be featured prominently in my thoughts...along with where I saw her."

"Now, hold on a minute. That's blackmail."

Ethan held out his hand.

Grumbling under his breath, Joe put his car keys in Ethan's palm.

"Thanks. You might as well change the oil while my car's here. I'll pay you when I pick it up tonight."

He whistled the "Battle Hymn of the Republic" as he made his getaway through the garage.

An amiable records clerk was a P.I.'s best friend. Some records were online these days, but a lot weren't. Ethan's second stop after ditching Claudia was the Middlesex County Courthouse, that having been Norblusky's county of residence before he'd dropped out of sight.

Unfortunately, at this courthouse he didn't have a friendly clerk. All he had was Lenny—creaky, cantankerous, slow and sour. But bribable, at least. Tickets to the next Celtics home game usually kept him cooperative.

It was his own fault he was stuck with Lenny. Back in his workaholic period he'd briefly dated the clerk who used to help him here. Julia had claimed she wasn't interested in a relationship, just some mutual fun. She'd been slim and pretty and good company, if too talkative—she'd talked before, during and after sex. But the sex itself had been good, and he'd thought they were doing fine on the mutual fun arrangement.

On their fifth date, she'd spent the afterglow talking about marriage. She hadn't appreciated his reaction. Since she talked at work, too, none of the female clerks would lift a ledger for him these days.

Julia had also been blond. Tall, slim and blond. Like Bianca. Like Claudia, dammit. Ethan scowled at the microfiche reader. He had no sense when it came to women packaged that way.

At least he'd taken care of one potential complication. If he ever saw the tall, slim, blond Ms. Barone again, he'd be too busy ducking to get into any trouble with her.

It was after four when he left the courthouse, too late to hit the Suffolk County records. He'd mostly drawn negatives in Middlesex—no record of any lawsuits, no marriages or divorces, no property taxes paid. He'd struck it lucky in one way, though. Five years ago Norblusky had registered his will with the county. It left all his worldly goods to his sister, Sophia Anne Lamont. Best of all, Ethan had an address for her, one that matched a Charles Lamont in the phone book.

He whistled a tune from *The Little Mermaid* as he headed for Joe's car. The sun was still around but on its way down, washing the streets with that slanted, golden light that always made him think of faded photographs and Oreos. He used to slam in through the back door after school, hoping for Oreos. His mother hadn't been much for baking, but she'd kept a package of cookies in the pantry just for him.

Until he was nine, that is. Everything had changed that year.

Grief fades, he thought as he climbed in Joe's little Toyota. Like old photographs left out in the sun, the years gradually blur even the harshest colors. What was left was a gentle sort of melancholy, not unpleasant. Kind of a dark gold feeling, like the late afternoon light. He started the car.

He decided to head back to his office, where he could use his computer to access some of the online records now that he had Norblusky's social security number. He'd give Sophia Lamont a call later.

His office was in the North End, so he had to fight traffic. It was a bitch, but no worse than usual. But when he got there, his parking space was taken. By his own car. He had to park two blocks away.

Joe must have gotten his wires crossed. He'd been supposed to drive Ethan's car home and let Ethan pick it up later. The idiot probably panicked, Ethan thought as he headed up the stairs. Didn't want to explain to Cindy why he had Ethan's car. Poor guy was henpecked. Maybe Cindy had been confusing him with all that sensitivity stuff.

When he reached the top of the stairs he heard a woman's laugh. His heartbeat scrambled into double time. Oh, Lord. That explained it. Joe must have crumbled, let Claudia use the car. But why had she brought it here? And how had she gotten into his office?

The door was open. Claudia was there, all right, sitting on his desk with her legs crossed, one leg swinging. So was another of his cousins, a cop who moonlighted part-time for Ethan. Rick was standing too close to her, and he had a gleam in his eyes. Ethan knew that gleam.

''Ethan.'' Claudia smiled at him. ''Rick has been keeping me entertained while I waited for you. He's told me all your secrets.''

Her eyes were twinkling. And they crinkled at the

corners, too. He stopped, perplexed. She was furious, wasn't she? So why did she look pleased to see him?

He switched his glare to Rick.

"Hey, don't look at me like that. I don't even know all your secrets."

He knew enough. "You let her in."

Rick shrugged. He was younger than Ethan—too young for Claudia, dammit—and better-looking. He even had a dimple. "I was using your computer when she showed up. Finished my report on the Simmons surveillance—which, by the way, should be over now. Caught him at the motel with his side piece."

"Good work," Ethan said, but he was distracted. Just what had Rick told Claudia? "But it doesn't explain why Claudia is here."

"I guess I should have kicked her out. Shoved her down the stairs, maybe."

"It would take that to discourage her." He sighed and hung his coat on the coatrack.

She chuckled and shoved off his desk. "Don't look so worried. You were ready for me to throw things, weren't you? Pitch a fit? I like to win, but that doesn't mean I can't appreciate an opponent's moves when they're good. Yours was. You ditched me neatly, and without ever quite lying."

She sounded…admiring. He gave up on making sense of her. Obviously she was crazy. No point in arguing with a crazy woman. "Hope I haven't kept you waiting long."

"Less than an hour," she assured him. "I finished my end of the investigation a little faster than you handled yours. Or maybe I was luckier with traffic."

"You don't have an end of the investigation. Or a middle. Or any part in it at all."

"I didn't *think* you were listening." She shook her head. "I told you I was going to talk to Donna."

"Who's Donna?"

She gave him a patient look. "I told you. She runs the Meals-On-Wheels program. And her husband is some muckety-muck in the VFW, and Norblusky's application said he was a veteran. It seemed worth checking into. Donna put me in touch with someone from the post Norblusky belonged to, and *he* gave me the name of a friend of Norblusky's who told me that Norblusky has a sister."

He wasn't thrilled to learn she'd gotten the same lead he had. Petty of him, maybe, but there it was. "Yeah, I found her in the courthouse records. Sophia Lamont. I have her address and phone number."

"That's good. My contact didn't have that, or know her married name. Did you also find out about Norblusky's ex-wife?"

"His...ex-wife." Ethan kept his voice level. Barely. The lousy little rat bastard hadn't told anyone at Baronessa that he used to be married. He hadn't even had the courtesy to get married or divorced in Middlesex County, where Ethan would have found the record.

An ex-wife trumped a sister all to hell. Being full of grievances, former spouses were a lot more likely to help a P.I. find a skip than friends or family members. "No. I didn't know about her."

Claudia nodded. "I have her address and phone

number. She's agreed to talk to me.'' At last her smile took on an edge. ''Just to prove there are no hard feelings, I thought I'd see if you wanted to come along.''

Four

"You aren't going," Ethan said.

"Don't be ridiculous." The man didn't seem to realize she'd won. Claudia reached behind her for her purse and took out her lipstick and compact.

She would be gracious about her little triumph, she thought as she slicked Carnation Blush over her lips. Gloating was tacky. And she wasn't one to hold a grudge. He'd beat her fair and square earlier.

She had been upset, though. A little. Actually, it had…hurt. When she'd realized that he had tricked her—that he had no intention of ever seeing her again—it had stung. And that was unforgivably foolish. She snapped the compact closed. Good grief, the man had kissed her exactly once. They weren't dating. They weren't even friends. Friendly opponents, maybe, with a shift under way toward temporary colleagues. But he didn't owe her a thing.

Ethan was glaring at her. ''You'll give me this woman's name, address and phone number, and I'll keep your appointment.''

Hadn't he been paying attention at all? ''No, I won't.''

''Well, I'm out of here,'' Rick said cheerfully. ''Much as I'd like to see who draws first blood, I've got a date with my bed. I'm seven and a half hours behind on my sleep this week.''

Claudia smiled at him. Really, Rick had been most helpful. ''I'm so glad I had a chance to meet you, Rick.''

Ethan was eyeing his cousin suspiciously. Probably wondering about those secrets she'd mentioned. Rick had let some interesting things drop after Claudia hinted that she and Ethan were a couple.

''I need to see an accident report,'' Ethan said, and handed Rick a slip of paper. ''Just what's in the public records. You can get it faster than I can.''

''What accident?'' Claudia demanded.

''A produce truck spilled a load of habanero peppers, causing the Baronessa truck ferrying the gelato to the tasting to be stuck in traffic. It's in the report your cousin gave me.''

Claudia frowned. She needed to see that report.

''Well, kiddies, I've got to be going,'' Rick said, giving Claudia a wink. ''Don't want to keep my bed waiting. Play nice while I'm gone.'' He closed the door behind him.

Claudia hitched herself back up on the desk. Negotiating time. ''You have a large family,'' she observed. ''I know what that's like. Rick told me about some of them.''

"Never mind about my family. Claudia, you can't go on this interview."

"You look just like Nicholas when he's laying down the law. All steely and determined. It's very attractive."

He huffed and ran a hand over his hair. "Look, turning up the ex-wife was great, a real coup. But there's more to questioning someone than smiling while you verbally pound them until they break."

"I don't know why you keep assuming I'm stupid. Surely it's not just my hair color. Maybe you think only people with paid jobs have brains?" She shook her head sadly. "Ethan, listen to me. I'm not going to tell you how to find Norblusky's ex-wife, and staring holes through me won't make me change my mind. Either you go with me, or I go on my own."

He paced a few steps, stopped and turned. "You don't seem to realize that this perp, whoever he is, may be dangerous. The gelato tampering was small change. But it didn't accomplish whatever he wanted, so he moved up to the big time. Arson."

"Good grief. Norblusky's ex-wife isn't a suspect. I don't *think* she's going to shoot me if she doesn't like the questions I ask."

"For all you know, Norblusky is hiding out at her place. Maybe she agreed to talk to you to find out what you know. Maybe Norblusky is the one who wants you within reach, not his ex."

A chilling thought. She rubbed her arms and smiled. "Wow. You have a lurid imagination. Still, that proves it would be better if you went with me, doesn't it?"

"Stop doing that!" He grabbed her arms and yanked her off his desk.

"Wh-what? Stop what?" Dappled eyes, she was thinking, her head tilted back to blink up at them. Like leaves and dirt and the shady spots beneath a tree…his lips were too thin, though. Especially when he was angry like this. Thin and hard.

"Don't smile that way when you're hurt or frightened. It makes me crazy."

Something was surely making him crazy. Unfortunately, it seemed to be catching. She could taste her own heartbeat as it pumped summery sweetness through her veins. "Some people face fear with curses. I prefer smiling at it."

"Well, don't." His hands slid down her arms, stopping at her cocked elbows. His thumbs began making little circles, barely felt through the thick wool of her sweater. "I don't like it."

"Why not?" She found herself leaning into him.

"Because." His gaze flicked to her mouth. He dragged it back up to her eyes. "There's a reason. I'll think of it in a minute. Something to do with…fear."

"I see." She saw *him.* Expressive eyebrows drawn down in confusion now, not anger. Tricky, two-toned eyes intent on her, their pupils pleasure-gorged just from standing near her. A hard mouth pulled in a thin, denying line.

It would soften, she knew it would, if she kissed it.

So she did.

Ethan resisted like crazy. For about as long as it takes to flip a switch from Off to On, he fought her advances. Then he wrapped himself around her and ate her up.

Oh, my. This man didn't need direction or encouragement—he would take everything she would let him have, and then some. Thrilled, Claudia gave herself up to sensation.

He tasted of coffee and subtler flavors, a blend that was only Ethan. She went exploring, wanting to know all his tastes, his scents—like here, along his jaw, where whiskers roughened her mouth's journey.

But he wanted her mouth, and he wanted it right now. He claimed it and spun her in an awkward two-step that ended with her back pressed against something smooth and cool and hard. File cabinets? With himself pressed against her front—warm and hard and not at all smooth.

Ethan undertook his own explorations. His hand was warm and callused on the skin of her stomach and, a moment later, on her breast. Desire skidded over her, landing with a jolt to burn low in her belly. He plucked at her nipple.

Claudia's hands clenched in his hair. Such wonderful hair. How could she have thought it ordinary? It was thick as a mink's pelt, warm from his body's heat.

He pushed up her sweater. Her front-clasp bra dangled loose. He looked at her naked breasts and smiled.

A door slammed. Then a female voice called Ethan's name.

They jumped apart.

"Ahh..." He ran a hand over his hair, pacing away to stop in front of his desk. "That was—I didn't—

we agreed, dammit. Are you self-destructive or something?''

''Sorry,'' she gasped, reaching frantically under her sweater for the loose ends of her bra. There. She jerked the two sides together, hooked them, and bent to get her breasts seated properly, straightened and pulled her sweater down. ''Yes, I am. Romantically, that is, not in any other way.''

''Claudia?'' His eyebrows twitched and his eyes went dreadfully soft. ''What do you—''

The office door slammed open. Bianca Conti stood framed in the doorway, a tall blond goddess with her hands on her Armani-clad hips and a sneer on her face. ''What do you think you're doing?'' she demanded.

Claudia, off to the right and out of Bianca's line of sight, stifled a hysterical giggle.

Ethan grimaced. ''Have you ever heard of knocking?''

Bianca, single-minded as ever, stomped up to him. ''How dare you prey on my father? God only knows how you convinced him to hire you. I know what you're up to, don't think I don't! You mean to frame my family for everything those stupid Barones have brought upon themselves. I won't have it, Ethan! I won't let you do it!''

''Bianca,'' Ethan said dryly, ''I think you already know Claudia, don't you?''

Claudia cleared her throat delicately.

Bianca whirled and shrieked.

Claudia smiled at her. ''Hello, Bianca. Love the slacks. Did you find them at Bergstrom's? They had some just like that on sale last week.'' Translation: *So sorry you have to buy at half price these days.*

''These are Armani,'' Bianca informed her coldly. ''What are you doing here?''

Kissing the socks off of your ex-husband was probably not a tactful response. ''Isn't it obvious? I'm looking out for my family's interests. Seeing that your father is the one who hired him.''

Ethan sighed, leaned against his desk and crossed his arms ''Which, I'd like to point out, you didn't know until Bianca came storming in here and blurted it out.''

''Oh, that's right, blame me!'' Bianca rounded on him again. ''You always have. For everything.''

''I stopped blaming anything on you years ago. I don't need to anymore.''

A small silence fell. For the first time, Bianca looked uncertain.

Claudia suppressed a sigh. Bianca was such a drama queen, accustomed to the idea that the world revolved around her—or ought to. No doubt it was disconcerting to discover that her ex-husband didn't spend his time hating her for having ruined his life. ''It was all a long time ago,'' she said kindly, coming forward to pat Bianca on the shoulder.

Bianca looked highly suspicious. ''I would think you'd have the courtesy to leave when it's obvious Ethan and I would like to have a private conversation.''

''Amazing the way you still know what he wants after all these years.'' One thing she had to say for Bianca: she was not a Pillow Woman. Didn't that say something about Ethan, too? She turned to him.

‘‘Now, about that interview. Did you want to go with me?’’

He straightened quickly. The light in his eyes looked a lot like gratitude. ‘‘Definitely. We’d better leave now if we don’t want to be late.’’

‘‘Right. We’d better hit the road. Traffic sucks, you know.’’

You never saw horizons in the city, Claudia mused. The sun had set, but its passage was marked as much by light as by darkness. Artificial light. As Ethan’s big Buick headed down Huntington, the city slipped into its night wear like a middle-aged lady dressing up in her bangles and glitter. Streetlights winked on; lights glowed in windows and doors, on billboards and neon signs. Brash swaths of light flooded the concrete at gas stations, supermarkets and malls, while headlights beaded the streets.

City lights. They made it hard to spot the point when day crossed over into night, just as city buildings hid the horizon. But that didn’t mean those lines didn’t exist.

She’d given Ethan the name and address of Norblusky’s ex-wife, who lived way out in Brookline. Beyond that, she had no idea what to say to him.

What was wrong with her?

Claudia had always had a healthy sex drive, but this—this mindlessness that overtook her when Ethan touched her was new. Frightening. She’d been completely out of control. And she’d loved it. If Bianca hadn’t come storming up the stairs….

She grimaced.

Ethan glanced at her. ‘‘Something wrong?’’

He had that gentle tone in his voice. The one he'd used when she'd admitted to being romantically impaired. She didn't like it. It made her want to tell him…things.

Well, there *was* something she had to tell him. She took a deep breath, thinking about horizons and crossing unseen lines. She'd stepped over one. "About what happened in your office—"

"We aren't going to discuss that. Besides, nothing happened. We stopped."

"Right." Never mind what might have happened if his ex-wife hadn't chosen that moment to show up. An image flashed through Claudia's mind involving Ethan's desk and a serious lack of trousers on her part. She flushed. "We stopped. But you should know—"

"Look, I really don't want to go through any post-game analysis. There's no point. No offense, but you aren't my type."

"And you aren't mine," she said through gritted teeth. "But what I'm *trying* to say is that I'm seeing someone else right now, so you don't need to worry about any, um, repeats."

"Oh. Right. That's excellent." He gave one sharp nod. His finger tapped out an agitated rhythm on the steering wheel. "If you're seeing someone, you had no business kissing me that way."

"Neil and I…" No, she did not owe him any explanations. "Are none of your business," she finished, but immediately lost the high moral ground by adding, "Besides, I thought you didn't want to discuss it."

He took that in grim silence. She rewarded his forbearance by prying delicately. "Actually, I was thinking about Bianca."

"Thinking about her has that effect on me, too. Puckers me up like a lemon."

Poor Bianca. "She doesn't seem your type."

"Now, there's an understatement. I was pretty young when we met. Easy to mistake the razzle-dazzle of sex for something lasting."

"So that's all it was? Sexual attraction?" He'd been attracted to a strong, if obnoxious, woman in the past....

"It sure wasn't because we had so much in common. I've learned my lesson, though. No more society twits."

Society twit. Had he meant that as an oblique comment on their recent grab-and-pant session? Which had been entirely mutual, dammit. She frowned at his unrevealing profile. "Having a common background is no guarantee of romantic bliss. If things go wrong, it just makes the disaster more public."

He glanced at her. His face still wasn't giving much away, but his mouth softened. "I guess you'd see it that way."

"Mutual respect is the most important element."

"I won't argue with that."

"I'm not talking about Drake, you understand."

"No?"

"I'm talking about..." She sighed. "All right, about him, but not just him. I'm extrapolating from more than one datum."

"You're what?'

"Extrapolating. It means—"

"I know what it means. Believe it or not, they use

words of more than one syllable at Harvard Business School. Even football grunts are expected to learn all kinds of tricky language like *collateral* and *market-based economics.* But I never thought I'd hear a woman *extrapolate* about relationships. Women are always going on about feelings, not logic.''

''Well.'' She shrugged, uncomfortable. ''I'm not especially feminine. My instincts about intimate relationships are undependable, so I make do with logic.''

''You're kidding, right?'' His glance was quick and surprised, but that faded into puzzlement. ''You aren't. You really don't think you're feminine. But that's stupid. Just look at you.''

She shook her head, her mouth twisting wryly. ''Protective camouflage. I learned how to blend in a long time ago. It's not really fake,'' she assured him. ''I enjoy clothes and makeup and all that. But that's frosting. Putting frosting on a basketball doesn't make it a cake.''

He chuckled. ''Wouldn't make it easy to shoot hoops, either. Not that you remind me in any way, shape or manner of a basketball.''

''Glad to hear it. How about a steamroller? That's what my brother Daniel calls me—a steamroller in white gloves.''

He didn't say a word.

''I can tell you agree.'' His expression made her grin. ''For heaven's sake, it's not an insult. I'm very goal-oriented, and I generally do accomplish what I set out to do. That's not a feminine trait, but I'm certainly not apologizing for it.''

He was frowning as if she'd posed some difficult

problem and insisted that he solve it. She wondered if she should reassure him again that none of this bothered her, but perhaps he'd think she was protesting too much.

How had they gotten off on such a stupid topic? "About Ed Norblusky—"

He spoke right over her. "What was his name again?"

"Who?" she asked, at sea. "Norblusky?"

"No, this man you're seeing."

"Uh, Neil. Neil Braddock."

"And Neil doesn't think you're feminine?"

"Well...I'm sure... That is, he appreciates me the way I am. He doesn't care if I'm feminine or not." Neil *did* like and appreciate her. She appreciated him, too, even if...well, Stacy was wrong, that was all. And Ethan's opinion didn't count. He didn't even know Neil. Her voice turned tart. "I can't imagine why I'm telling you any of this."

"Mmm," he said absently, and shook his head. "I don't get it. How can a woman who damned near ignited my shorts with a kiss think she isn't sexy?"

Something jumped right up in her throat and stuck there. Some warm, alarmed feeling. Claudia swallowed, looked out the window, ran a hand over her hair and eventually was able to speak. "Thank you. I think. But 'sexy' and 'feminine' aren't the same thing."

"Is this some kind of female code?" he asked, his eyes narrowing.

"What?"

"You know, like mauve. Women all know what mauve is. Is this 'sexy but not feminine' business something you could say to ten women and they'd know what you meant? Because I can tell you right now, it doesn't make sense to a man."

A bubble of laughter unstuck whatever had been clogging her throat. "Maybe it is. I hadn't thought of it that way." She cocked her head to one side. "You seem to know a lot about women."

"Cousins." The car slowed as he turned off on a residential street. "My life is littered with cousins, and what do you know—about half of them grew up to be women. They all want to give me advice."

She grinned. "How many cousins do you have?"

"Enough for two football teams, with a few left over."

"Good grief. I thought I had a big family. Are you sure you aren't Italian?"

"That's one of the few things I'm not. Irish and English on my father's side, but my mother was a real Heinz 57—Welsh, Swedish, Scottish, Austrian, German, and her great-great-grandmother on her mother's side was supposedly half Apache, half African. Family legend says that *her* father was an escaped slave," he added, "but my aunt Violet—she's into genealogy—has never been able to find any records to confirm that. Frustrates the hell out of her."

"My goodness. You're a walking melting pot."

"Now, there's a sexy image."

She was still smiling as they pulled to a stop in front of a small frame house flanked by overgrown evergreens. Two cement steps led to a cement stoop, where a yellow porch light glowed by the door. "I can see why you haven't remarried, then, if you're looking for someone from a similar background. There can't be too many Welsh-Irish-Swedish-English-Austrian-German-African-Apache people around.''

''You left out Scottish. And that's not what I meant.'' He turned off the engine and opened his door.

She climbed out, too. ''Oh, by background, do you mean social standing? Or money? Maybe that's what you think you should have in common with a woman. You want her to come from the same financial background. So do you just guess about that, or do you ask your dates how much money their parents have?''

He joined her on the sidewalk. ''I have them fill out a questionnaire. If things get serious I ask for old tax returns, just to be sure. You think we could stop talking about my personal life now? We need to set some rules for this interview.''

''You mean *you* want to set some rules.''

He grinned and took her elbow. ''Think of it like dancing, honey. I lead, you follow.''

Five

Two hours later, Ethan was buckling up again and thinking about supper. By the time he dropped Claudia off and reached his own apartment, it would be too late to cook. Which meant fast food. Again.

Maybe he didn't have to drop her off, though. Maybe she'd like to talk about the case over—whoa. Even if she didn't get the wrong idea, his libido would. It already had. Ever since he saw her breasts…

He started the car's engine and tried to tamp down his own.

Claudia announced, "I'm going with you tomorrow."

"How did I know you'd say that?" Ethan shook his head in amazement. "I'm developing powers. Quick, pick a number between one and ten."

"Two thousand."

"You did say you weren't good at following instructions."

Claudia hadn't been the pain in the butt he'd expected. She had good instincts about when to prompt, when to sit back and listen and—most surprising—when to let Ethan direct the conversation.

In fact, they'd made a good team. It was disconcerting.

"You're good at getting people to talk," she told him.

"I hardly ever need the rubber hose these days." Eating alone was sounding less appealing all the time. "You were pretty good, too. You even stayed quiet sometimes."

"Contrary to popular opinion, I don't *have* to be in charge of everything. I step in when something needs fixing. The interview didn't. You knew what you were doing."

"Hmm." The warm approval in her voice made him want to flex a muscle or two, and see if she approved of that, too. "I have something that needs fixing."

She shot him a suspicious look.

He laughed. "Not that. I'm having trouble getting in touch with your brother. Can you set up a meeting for me?"

"I have two brothers, you know. I suppose you mean Derrick? I don't see why you need to talk to him. We're on Norblusky's trail now. We know his most recent employer, plus the names of some of his drinking buddies."

Ethan drummed his fingers on the steering wheel. Logic told him to lie, but dammit, he was starting to like her. "Norblusky's a good lead, but we don't know how he's connected. Maybe he isn't. So I have to keep turning over stones to see what's under them. Derrick is in charge of quality control, and he was Norblusky's boss."

He waited for her indignation to spew out all over him, her demands to know what he was talking about. But when he glanced at her she was sitting very straight, looking worried.

Ah, hell. He didn't like seeing that soft, anxious look on her face. It made him feel the way he had when she insisted it didn't matter one bit to her that she wasn't feminine. He grabbed another subject, wanting to distract her. "How did this feud between the Contis and the Barones get started, anyway? And what's the significance of Valentine's Day?"

"What? Oh." She shook her head slightly, as if returning from some distant place. "I'm surprised you don't know. Didn't Sal Conti tell you about it?"

"He said it was ancient history, and that no one believed in curses these days. Naturally that made me curious, but he didn't want to talk about it. The newspapers haven't been much help. There was an article in the *Herald* that mentioned Valentine's Day, a curse and star-crossed lovers, but it was long on speculation and short on facts."

"I saw that article. Tabloid journalism at its best. I'm not sure there *were* any facts in it. They didn't even get the curse right."

"You mean there really is a curse?"

"Certainly. Do you want to hear the story?"

He nodded.

"Long ago and not so far away, a young man fell

in love. He was poor, of course—all the best heroes start out that way. But these lovers weren't star-crossed. The young man's sweetheart loved him, too, and one sunny Valentine's Day they ran off and got married."

"Let me guess. These two young lovers were your grandparents, Marco Barone and Angelica...I don't remember her maiden name."

"Good guess. Anyway, the young lovers achieved their happy ending, or so it seemed. But like so many things, it came at a price."

"The curse?" he asked wryly.

"Something more important. Friendship. You see, back then the Contis were well off and the Barones were poor. But the families had been neighbors back in Sicily, so when Marco came to this country, it was under the Contis' sponsorship. He was their godson. They gave him a job in their restaurant, where he met Angelica, who was working there as the dessert chef. Her specialty—" she paused dramatically "—was gelato made from an old family recipe."

"And that was the basis for Baronessa? Angelica's gelato recipe?"

"You've got it."

"So the feud's really about money. The Contis felt wronged when Marco stole Angelica and her gelato from them."

"Oh, it goes deeper than that. The Contis' son, Vincent—Sal Conti's father—had been sweet on Angelica himself. He and his parents all expected her to marry him—and then she eloped with my grandfather, whom the Contis thought was going to marry their daughter, Lucia."

"Oh, ho. Betrayed love all over the place. Have we arrived at the curse?"

"Yes. Lucia Conti cursed Valentine's Day for her rival and her faithless lover. And a year later, Angelica miscarried their first child…on Valentine's Day."

"Coincidence."

"Probably."

"Oh, come on. You don't believe in curses."

"Not really. Only…well, a lot of bad stuff has happened to various Barones on Valentine's Day. My uncle Luke was stolen from the hospital nursery on that day over forty years ago. I think most of us stiffen up in spite of ourselves when February 14 rolls around."

"The tasting was scheduled for Valentine's Day."

"I suspect someone was trying to make a point: 'See, Ma, no curse!' Only it backfired. The one person I know was pleased was old Lucia Conti. She never forgave my grandfather for marrying someone else. If I could see any way that she could have tampered with the gelato, she'd be my prime suspect. That old woman has built her life around her curse, like the thorn thickets that grew up around Sleeping Beauty's castle. She never married, and she *looks* like a witch now, all long, stringy hair and hoarse cackling."

That startled a laugh from him. He'd seen Lucia Conti. "I guess her appearance does lend a superficial authority to the curse."

"Yes." A thoughtful line formed between her eyebrows. "But even though I could imagine the old woman cackling as she peppered our gelato, I can't picture her or any of the others burning down the plant. We—the Contis and my family—haven't always played nice with one another, but it's been little stuff. One-upmanship. Not arson."

"Hmm. A couple of people in your family have mentioned the Contis as suspects."

"Not everyone in my family has good sense. Which is why Sal Conti hired you, I assume." She thought that over. "You know, this feud has gone on too long."

He grinned as he came to a stop at the light. "You say that as if you thought you could do something about it."

"Not right away, I suppose. Priorities. Speaking of which..." All of a sudden she unfastened her seat belt, twisted up onto her knees and leaned over the back of the seat.

"What the—sit down!" He grabbed for her, got a fistful of sweater and tugged.

"You're going to stretch it all out of shape," she told him severely.

He could get a better grip and yank her back down in the seat, but he couldn't think of any way to keep her there. Ethan sighed, let go of her sweater and glanced over his shoulder. "You want to tell me why you're ransacking my files?"

"*Do* pay attention to the road, please. My position's a little precarious and I'd hate...ah, here it is." She righted herself, a red binder in one hand.

The report Nicholas had given him. That was what she'd gone after. "It's a little dark in here for reading."

"I have lamps at my place."

"But I'm not going to let you take my only copy."

Inspiration struck. ‘‘We could stop somewhere, grab a bite to eat. Someplace well lit, so you could read.’’

Claudia tapped the report with one finger. ‘‘A business dinner?’’

‘‘Of course.’’ Pears. That was what her breasts made him think of—pretty white pears, blushing at their tips.

‘‘You going to charge it to your client?’’ She grinned. ‘‘I’d like to see Sal Conti’s face if you do. I don’t think a Conti has bought a meal for a Barone since Marco worked at Antonio’s.’’

‘‘I’ll take that to mean yes. Any suggestions for where to go?’’

‘‘Paprikás is close to my place, and the light’s good enough to read by. You can park in my space. Turn right at the light.’’

‘‘Okay.’’ It’s just a dinner, he told himself as he followed her directions. No big deal. He hadn’t realized how sick he was of eating alone, though. The prospect of sitting across from Claudia while he ate had him smiling in anticipation.

She’d be good company, too, not just good scenery, though heaven knows she was that. He wondered what she’d make of the report. Claudia’s brain might not travel along predictable routes, but she was plenty bright. He found he was looking forward to discussing it with her, and frowned slightly. There was a lot he shouldn’t discuss, dammit. Her brother, for example. If she knew what he was beginning to suspect about Derrick, she’d lob her dinner at him instead of eating it.

A pang struck, sharp and unexpected. If he was right about Derrick, Claudia was going to be hurt. He wished there was some way…hold it, he told himself sternly. No call to get all protective. If ever there was a woman who could handle herself just fine without a man running interference for her, it was Claudia Barone. She was strong all the way down.

But *strong* didn't equal *invulnerable.* She could be hurt—*had* been hurt, he thought, remembering a fleeting look he'd glimpsed in her eyes a few times. Stubborn, prideful woman. She preferred to hide her hurt, and he could understand that. But that didn't make the pain less real.

Damn that brother of hers.

A meal is no big thing, Claudia assured herself as they walked the block from her parking space to the restaurant she'd suggested. People eat together all the time. Shoot, she'd bet not a single couple at the restaurant would fall all over each other in the middle of their chicken paprikash.

"No, it doesn't make sense," Ethan announced suddenly, just as if they'd been arguing the whole way. "There's no earthly reason to rent parking if you don't own a car."

She glanced at him and chuckled. Ever since he found out her parking space was available because she didn't have a car, he'd been all bent out of shape. He could not get his mind around the concept. "Not owning a car doesn't mean I never need parking. My space came in handy tonight, didn't it?"

"You rent parking so other people can use it?"

"I like to know my guests can park safely."

He brooded on that for a moment. "But what if you want to drive up to the Cape for the weekend?"

"I rent a car or go with someone who has one." She patted his arm. "I can tell it's a shock to your system, but I find it simpler not to keep a car. It's not that big a deal, Ethan."

"But..." He shook his head. "I just don't get it."

"That's obvious. Look, here we are."

Paprikás was one of Claudia's favorite guilty pleasures. The food was fabulous, it was within walking distance of her apartment—and not one item on the menu could possibly be mistaken for low fat or low calorie. It was just the type of place that would appeal to Ethan, she suspected.

Unfortunately, it appealed to a lot of others, too. The foyer was full of people waiting on tables.

"I am sorry, Miss Barone," Henry told her regretfully. "There will be a short wait. Would you and your escort care for a glass of wine?"

"Maybe some of that nice merlot I had last time. Thank you. Ethan?"

"Ah..." He'd been gazing off to her left. His attention returned to her face. "Nothing for me, thanks." He took her elbow.

She turned her head, wondering what he'd been staring at. "What was so— Ethan! Quit yanking on me."

"We need to get out of the traffic lane."

"In case you hadn't noticed, we're elbow to elbow in here, and there *is* no spot that's..." Her voice drifted off. The couple immediately to her left moved off, and she spotted a familiar profile.

Drake. Tall, blond, lean as a whip and as elegant as ever. His suit was dove-gray silk. His movements were quick, brimming with barely suppressed energy. He shone brightly, Drake did, and he knew it. He had a way of making those around him fade into the background.

She'd wondered sometimes if that was what he'd disliked most about her. She didn't fade.

"So what do you recommend?" Ethan asked a shade too loudly.

"Hmm? Oh, the chicken paprikash. It's the house specialty." How wearisome, she thought. How annoying. She still felt that same little clutch around her heart when she saw Drake. Not lust or liking or infatuation, certainly—just the sad little ghost of foolish dreams.

"Is it spicy?" Ethan asked. "I like it hot."

"Oh..." She gave him a distracted smile. "It's spicy, but not mouth-burning. You'll like it." She knew one of the men with Drake. Will was the kind of attorney the jokes were made for—slick as slime and very expensive. The other man was a stranger.

Just then the man she didn't know looked right at her and said something. And the other two snickered.

Why, they were talking about her! And *laughing.* Claudia took a quick, involuntary step toward them, then stopped. What could she do? She didn't have a tub of ice cream handy.

She could hear snatches of their conversation now.

"...bet she liked...in charge in bed," the college buddy was saying. "Women like that..."

Drake didn't once look at her, but damn him, he knew she was there. He spoke just loudly enough to be sure she would hear. "Well, she did like to be on top. Which is all right once in a while, but every time?''

More laughter.

''Excuse me a minute,'' Ethan said to her.

''Ethan? Wait, Ethan, what are you doing?'' She grabbed at his arm, but somehow he was already out of reach, though he didn't seem to be moving fast. He sauntered up to the three men and tapped Drake on the shoulder.

Drake turned, making a show of surprise and smiling to show off his perfect teeth. ''Yes?''

''You're talking about the lady I'm with.''

Oh, God. Ethan was going to punch someone. Claudia didn't know if she was more thrilled or appalled.

Drake's smile turned sharp. ''Detected that, did you, Mallory?''

''That's what I do, Anderson. Detect things.'' Ethan gave him a sleepy smile. ''I'm detecting a bad smell right now. You say Claudia always wanted to be on top?'' He shook his head sadly. ''I'm surprised you'd come right out and admit that to your friends. Hey, did you know you've got a little spot here?'' He brushed at Drake's lapel.

Drake looked annoyed. ''Keep your hands to yourself.''

''I don't think it's gravy.'' Ethan tilted his head consideringly. ''Maybe wine? Like I was saying…could be that your friends don't know Claudia. They might not realize that she only takes over when something, ah, needs fixing.''

''If you're trying, in your clumsy way, to imply—''

"No, no. I'm not *implying* anything. I'm saying that I know from personal experience that Claudia is perfectly willing to let someone else handle things—if he knows what he's doing." Ethan gave Drake a friendly nod. "Better get that stain taken care of before it sets." He turned away.

"Listen, you—" Drake grabbed Ethan's arm.

And Ethan spun back around lightly and stood quite still, balanced in a way that was somehow ominous, like a thunderhead piled up high and dark overhead. And looking eager—and not at all friendly.

He didn't say another word.

Drake's friends hustled him away, right out the door.

Claudia's heart was pounding. Her chest felt funny. That was…that was so…she didn't have words for how she felt. She walked up to Ethan, who was looking rather regretful that his opportunity had been removed. "Would you have hit him?" she asked.

"Only if he threw the first punch. I was kind of hoping…" He huffed out a breath. "I guess you're mad. But damned if I'm going to apologize. The rat bastard needs to learn to keep his lip zipped."

"I'm not mad."

"You're not?" Some of the tension in his shoulders eased.

"No, that was…nice." No one had ever come to her defense that way before. She was the strong one, the one who looked out for others. It never occurred to people that she might need help herself. And she didn't, not really, but it was lovely to have someone charge to the rescue.

Ethan had made *Drake* out to be the one who was sexually impaired.

A grin broke out all over Claudia's face. "I misspoke. That wasn't nice. It was great. *Better* than melted ice cream."

Six

"So what do you think?" Claudia asked, holding up both dresses. "The blue or the black?"

"I think you should turn the TV down," Stacy said.

"Then I wouldn't be able to hear it. The Patriots are playing, for heaven's sake."

"Football." Stacy was disgusted. She took a moment to inspect the tortilla chips in the bowl in her lap, carefully selected the biggest one and then dipped it gingerly into the salsa.

"If you're just going to dampen one corner of the chip, why bother?"

"I like it this way. Where's Neil taking you?"

"To some foreign film. Dinner first."

"Better watch out or he'll take you to a sushi bar. Neil likes sushi."

"And you know this because...?"

"He told me. Remember when you were late getting back from the board meeting of that hospice organization you're reorganizing? You asked me to meet him here and keep him entertained." She cautiously dipped another chip in the salsa. "We talked."

"He did suggest sushi. I thought Indian food sounded better. I haven't eaten a good curry in ages." She studied the two dresses and put the blue one back in the closet. Then she pulled out her emerald silk pajamas.

Well, *not* pajamas, technically. The outfit was actually full-cut evening slacks with an abbreviated top that buttoned up the front, though not terribly high up the front. It made her feel deliciously naughty, as if she were wearing her pj's in public. If this didn't provoke Neil into more than a good-night kiss, nothing would. She started to rehang the black dress.

"Wear the black," Stacy said without looking up. "You look smashing in the green silk, but the foreign film crowd always wears black. You'd stand out like a sore thumb. And that would make Neil uncomfortable."

Claudia sighed. And put back the pajamas. "Are you here to give me moral support or a hard time?"

"Actually, I came to park my leftovers and stayed to eat your chips. The wardrobe advice is a bonus."

Stacy's refrigerator had quit working that afternoon, so she'd brought most of its contents over to Claudia's. "I should charge you rent." Claudia frowned at the black dress. "There's nothing wrong with liking sushi. *You* like sushi."

"Love it. My taste buds haven't been destroyed by hot peppers the way yours have."

"Romantic compatibility is not based on liking the same foods."

"I'll bet Neil isn't watching the game right now."

No, he wouldn't be. But Ethan probably was. They'd argued about it. When Claudia had said that the other team's new wide receiver would give the Patriots a hard time, he'd insisted the man was overhyped and too new to be dependable. Pigheaded man.

Was he was watching the game alone, or with some of his many cousins? Or a woman?

None of my business, she told herself firmly. "I am not in the mood for black," she announced, and hung up the black dress and retrieved the dark blue one. It was a long sheath with a mandarin collar, appliqued at the hem and one hip with yellow flowers, and slit to within an inch of decency on one side.

A sudden roar from the television had her tossing the dress on the bed and racing for the living room. The announcer was hoarse and the crowd was on their feet. Dammit, what had happened?

Thank heavens for instant replay. The football soared up, arced down—and landed in the wide receiver's hands. He streaked for the goal line.

"Yes!" Claudia yelled, and pumped her fist in the air.

Stacy wandered out of the bedroom, the bag of chips in one hand, and gave Claudia an odd look. "I know you're a lot more up on football than I am, but aren't you cheering for the wrong team?"

''I'm not exactly *cheering* for them. I've got a bet on.''

''You bet against the Patriots?'' She clapped a hand to her chest. ''Call 911. We have an emergency here.''

''I wouldn't do that! I bet on the point spread. Ethan seems to think anyone with a uterus instead of gonads can't understand football. He practically patted me on the head and told me to go knit something when I offered an opinion on the other team's new running back.''

Stacy snickered. ''You offer opinions the way the Red Queen does—'off with his head!' Why were you arguing football with Ethan, anyway? I thought the only thing you had in common was the investigation. No personal relationship at all. At least that's what you've been claiming.''

''Oh, for heaven's sakes.'' Claudia's eyes drifted back to the set. They were setting up for the field goal. ''We were talking sports, not holding a deep, intimate conversation. The man used to play college ball. It's only natural the subject would come up.''

''Uh-huh. Well, to direct your mind to a subject of much less importance than football, is anything happening with the investigation?''

''We tracked down another of Norblusky's drinking buddies today, but he wasn't much help.'' So far they knew a whole lot of places that Ed Norblusky wasn't. ''But it's only been a few days. And tomorrow we talk to his sister. She might know something.''

''Why would she tell you if she does?''

‘‘Ethan’s good at getting people to talk.’’ She frowned at the TV. The kicker was in place.

‘‘You’ve been known to loosen a few lips, too. Out of sheer fear, if charm fails.’’

‘‘We’re a pretty good team. I got to play the bad cop today. I—damn!’’ The ball sailed up, pretty as could be, right between the goalposts.

‘‘You wanted them to get the touchdown, but not the field goal?’’

‘‘I don’t want them to win. And it messes up the point spread.’’ Absently Claudia sat on the couch. She held out a hand for the bag of chips. Stacy passed it to her, and she dug out one and crunched down, her eyes glued to the set.

‘‘Just what did you bet?’’

Her smile snuck out, a trifle smug. ‘‘Enough to make it interesting.’’

‘‘Oh, really? He can’t afford to bet enough to make it interesting to you.’’

‘‘Don’t be silly. Money isn’t interesting.’’

‘‘Claudia! You didn’t!’’

She laughed. ‘‘I bet gloating rights, Stacy, not sexual favors. A full day’s gloating rights for the winner. Did you really think I’d bet my body?’’

‘‘I think you want that man.’’

Well, yes. But she had it under control. She dug into the bag for another chip. ‘‘What did you do with the salsa?’’

‘‘It’s in the bedroom. Have you forgotten about Neil, or are you planning to entertain him in your undies?’’

Claudia yelped and dashed for the bedroom.

Stacy followed. She’d retrieved the chips and resumed her place on the bed, sitting cross-legged and watching Claudia with her owl eyes as she carefully dampened a chip in the spicy dip. "Tell me something. Why are you going out with a man you can completely forget from one moment to the next?"

Claudia had plenty of answers for that question. Good answers, too. She considered several of them as she slipped the blue dress over her head and zipped it up.

Neil was a genuinely nice man. He was gentle and cultured and they did, too, have things in common. She'd met him when she was setting up a visiting-nurse program for housebound AIDS patients on the south side. Neil ran a hospice in the area. He possessed such compassion, such a commitment to helping others…and no fire whatsoever. At least not with her.

If she could just get him to show a little passion, she thought for the hundredth time. If he'd just stop leaving it up to her how fast and how far their relationship went…

She could get him into bed. She knew that. But, dammit, she didn't want it to be all her idea. That had been her mistake in the past—going after a man before she knew for sure the feelings were mutual. And she'd rather stay home tonight and watch the game and eat chips and salsa with Stacy than go out with Neil, which didn't auger well for the success of her plan.

Especially since she couldn't watch it with the person she was *not* going to think about again tonight.

"'Dia? Was the question that hard to answer?"

Claudia grimaced and stepped into her shoes. "I

guess I'm going out with him because I said I would.''

Stacy nodded, accepting that. ''But why Monday night? You knew the Patriots were playing.''

''Neil's been out of town. He just got back.'' And she'd felt guilty. She'd put him off twice before he left for the weekend, caught up in the excitement of playing detective. ''Tell me something. Why are we friends? You and I don't have anything more in common than Neil and I do.''

''Sure we do. Mrs. Murphy and third grade. Camp Oaxita. Shane Hillbright.''

''You won the toss, but you didn't marry him.''

''My taste evolved beyond dimples. Besides, I think he turned out to be gay. And then there was Johnny.''

Claudia smiled reminiscently. ''Seventh grade. Your first boyfriend. My first fund-raising drive.''

''You made me help. The director of the National Red Cross sent you a personal letter of thanks.'' She smiled. ''London for our twenty-first birthdays.''

''Remember climbing to the top of St. Paul's?''

''I try not to. My thigh muscles still quiver in reproach if I think about it. How about sophomore English and Emily Dickinson?''

'''Hope is the thing with feathers....' I can't remember the rest.'' She paused. ''Pizza with anchovies.''

''No, that's still disgusting.''

Claudia laughed. ''All right, then. Chocolate.''

''Mimosas.''

''Charm bracelets.''

''Shoes.''

"Speaking of which..." Claudia glanced down. "Are these yours?"

Stacy peered over the end of the bed at Claudia's feet. "I think so."

The doorbell rang. Claudia looked at Stacy in sudden distress. "Why *am* I going out with Neil?"

"Because you said you would," Stacy said gently. "Go on, let him in. But you'll have to tell him soon that you can't see him anymore."

She sighed unhappily. "I know."

Ethan stared out at a gray, overcast day. The sky was the same color as the street. Even the traffic lights seemed subdued.

Claudia would be here soon. She had some kind of charity deal to attend this afternoon—a board meeting, so she couldn't put it off. They'd arranged for her to meet him at his office at nine o'clock.

That was why he'd be leaving at eight-thirty. If his cousin ever showed up.

The stairs creaked. A heavy, familiar tread. The office door opened. "Why so glum?" Rick asked.

Ethan continued to study the gray day outside. "You've been studying those 'expand your vocabulary' lists again."

"You look like your last lead just fell through. Must be a personal problem. I know it's not the game. The Patriots won."

Ethan grunted. "Not by enough."

"I thought you never bet on the point spread."

"Look, I didn't ask you to come in so we could discuss my mood. You mind if we talk business?"

Rick spread his arms. “Go right ahead. Though you briefed me last night, so it shouldn’t take long.”

“Something new came in.” He crossed to his desk and picked up the report that had come through on the fax machine last night.

Rick took it and started reading. His eyebrows drew together in a frown. “Some of this should not be available to private citizens.”

“Can I help it if people like to tell me things?” Actually, Ethan used an I.B.—an information broker—for this sort of thing. As Rick knew very well, but he pretended not to. I.B.’s sometimes took a casual approach to the legalities involved in gathering information.

Rick snorted and kept reading. Ethan moved behind his desk and sat, still facing the window. His chair creaked as he leaned back and propped his feet up on the space heater. Rick would go with Claudia to talk to Norblusky’s sister today while Ethan went to a part of the city no woman in her right mind would want to set foot in.

Not that Claudia was necessarily in her right mind. Ethan contemplated how to make sure she went with Rick if she showed up ahead of schedule. Best if he could convince her it was her own idea. Should he forbid her to talk to the sister, or was that too obvious?

Rick put the faxed report back on Ethan’s desk. “This Derrick Barone—he’s Claudia’s brother?”

“Yeah.”

“He’s been spending a lot lately, even for a lad with a trust fund. Yet he isn’t in debt. Not far enough in debt, anyway.'' He paused. ''He could have been bailed out by his father or his uncle.''

''Or any of several other relatives. But I don't think so.''

''You having one of your feelings?''

''I don't get feelings,'' Ethan said irritably. ''A hunch is a perfectly logical process. The subconscious puts together clues the conscious mind isn't aware of.''

''Whatever you say. But you think Derrick's involved in either the arson or the gelato tampering. Or both.''

Ethan sighed. ''Yeah.'' That was what his gut kept insisting—that Claudia's brother was in this right up to his white-collar neck.

''The police are concentrating on Norblusky.''

So was Claudia. ''He makes one hell of a great red herring.''

''He makes a pretty good suspect, too.'' Rick ticked points off on his fingers. ''He was driving the truck when the gelato was tampered with. He shot off his mouth about the Barones after being fired. And he's disappeared. Also, he worked at the plant long enough that he might have known how to circumvent the security.''

''Sure, Norblusky's a fine suspect, if you're willing to believe he's bright enough to have pulled off the gelato tampering. I'm not.''

Rick sat in the chair across from Ethan. ''You think he could have burned down an ice cream plant, but messing with a tub of ice cream was beyond him?''

''The arson seems to have been a pretty straightforward business. I'm not sure how the perp got in, but once in he just had to splash around a lot of gasoline, leave some trailers and light a match. But the gelato tampering was set up by someone who's watched too many *Mission: Impossible* reruns.''

Rick's lips twitched. ''A complicated operation, huh?''

''Someone arranged for a produce truck to lose its load on a street the Baronessa truck would take, causing a traffic jam. Someone climbed into the back of the truck and poured pepper juice on the gelato while the truck was stopped. That's two or three people involved. There's the driver of the produce truck, whoever actually poured the pepper juice, and probably Norblusky. The produce truck,'' Ethan added, ''was rented, using a bogus driver's license. Its driver has vanished, just like Norblusky.''

''Norblusky's not the *Mission: Impossible* type, I take it.''

Ethan snorted. ''More the Homer Simpson type.'' He paused. ''As far as I can tell, only three people knew the route the truck would take. Norblusky, who was driving it. His immediate boss, a guy name Aaron Fletcher. And *his* boss—Derrick Barone.''

Rick shook his head. ''For your sake, I hope it's Fletcher. You've checked him out?''

''I'm working on it.'' Without telling Claudia. It was getting tricky, keeping her aware of only half of what he was doing.

''Hmm. Makes things touchy for you. Is that why you want me to go with Claudia today?''

''Partly. I'd like to find Norblusky. If he thinks he's been set up to take the fall for arson, he might be willing to talk about who paid him to disappear.''

"Ah...I guess you've considered the possibility he could have been permanently 'vanished'."

"God, I hope not." Ethan ran a hand over his hair. If Claudia's brother was implicated in murder, she'd be devastated...and it didn't matter if she hated him for uncovering the truth, he told himself. They weren't involved. Once this case was closed he'd never see her again.

Ethan grimaced. "I have to proceed on the assumption he's still alive. If he isn't, your brothers on the force are a lot more likely to turn up his body than I am."

"True." After a moment he asked, "Have you told Claudia any of this?"

"What do you think?"

"I think she'd tip her brother off, either on purpose or inadvertently. Which would compromise your investigation. Which I guess answers my question." He shook his head. "You really like her, don't you? Aside from wanting to get her in bed, I mean."

"Yeah." He did like Claudia. He liked being with her, waiting to see what goofy thing she pulled next, or watching her take dead aim at some obstacle and mow it down. He liked listening to her. Looking at her. God, he loved that. Those incredible legs...but he also liked the way she held her head, erect on that slim little neck.

She did have a pretty neck. Graceful. She had a good walk for watching, too—brisk but sort of curvy, like a Slinky on fast forward. One of her eyeteeth was a little crooked, but it only showed when she opened that bee-stung mouth wide in a laugh. He liked the way she laughed.

He was in trouble. ''Hell,'' he said, and glanced at his watch as he shoved to his feet. ''I've got to get moving before she shows up. It's ten till nine, and the woman is obsessively punctual. I'd better use the back stairs to make sure I don't run into her.''

''Where are you going, anyway?''

''Boots called.'' Ethan grabbed an ankle-length black trench coat from the coatrack and shrugged into it. ''He says he has something for me.''

''Oh, hell, Ethan, he makes stuff up.''

''Sometimes. I guess none of your stoolies do that.'' Ethan shook his head, amazed, and reached for the hat that went with this getup. ''Wish I knew how to make them tell the truth all the time. They teach you how to do that at the academy?''

''Okay, okay. Just don't go see him alone. Wait till I get back and I'll go with you. Even cops cover that neighborhood in pairs.''

''The trick is not to look like a cop.'' He settled the hat on his head and reached for the walking stick.

''You definitely don't look like a cop. More like a pimp. And not a very successful one.''

''I have to blend in. I'm too big to go unnoticed.''

''Just be careful, will you?''

''I'm always careful.''

Claudia's heart pounded as she tiptoed back down the stairs, walking on the very edges to avoid creaks.

Imagine that. Ethan had planned to slip out without her. Naturally she had to know what he was trying to keep from her. Her lips curved as she reached the street. She'd watch his car, she decided. He always wanted to take his car—the man simply didn't believe in public transportation. Which meant she'd need a taxi. She looked around for one as she headed toward the store on the corner where Ethan always parked.

Why did everyone say eavesdroppers never heard anything good about themselves? Her smile widened, softened. Ethan liked her. That was what had stopped her right outside his office door, which had been ajar. Rick had been asking Ethan if he liked her.

He didn't just want to get her into bed. That was what Rick had said, and Ethan had agreed. He *liked* her.

Claudia was humming as she flagged down the taxi rounding the corner.

Seven

At least she wasn't lost, Claudia told herself as she stepped quickly along the broken sidewalk. She knew exactly where she was—walking up and down a single block in a section of the city that gave the word *slum* a bad name.

She wasn't alone on the street. The huddle of rags propped against one decaying building was really an old man. He smelled bad and he hadn't moved the entire time she'd been there, but she was fairly sure he was passed out, not dead.

Cars cruised by now and then, stereos blaring, the bass notes thrumming up through the soles of her feet. Across the street two older women walked quickly, their heads down.

And right in front of her three young men in "gangsta" pants and red-and-black jackets lounged in a wide doorway, passing around a funny-smelling cigarette. She hoped it was plain grass, not laced with PCP or something. One made her an extremely lewd offer as she hurried past. Another giggled. The third asked if she was deaf or something—didn't she hear them talking to her?

She walked faster.

Things could have been worse. It might have been dark, for example. No, even she wasn't idiot enough to have gotten out of the cab here at night. The cab probably wouldn't have even come here at night—he hadn't been too happy about bringing a fare here in the daytime. Claudia kept one hand inside her purse on her can of pepper spray.

If *only* that stupid cabdriver had agreed to stay!

She had never intended to leave the taxi without Ethan's large, comforting presence close at hand. She'd heard what Rick had said about the area, and a neighborhood where the police patrolled in pairs was not the spot for a woman alone to go strolling. She'd planned to follow Ethan to his destination, then get out when he parked his car. He would have been forced to take her with him.

Traffic, she mused, makes fools of us all.

Her cab had been slowed down by a creeping delivery van. She'd been stuck at a stop sign two blocks back when Ethan parked his big Buick. Which, she couldn't help noticing, blended in just fine here. She'd seen which building he went into.

This one. The three-story apartment building with unimaginative graffiti sprayed on one side of the door to welcome visitors. Some of the windows were boarded up.

She walked past it for the fourth time.

Exactly why she'd gotten out of the cab when the cabbie refused to circle the block, she couldn't say. It had seemed reasonable at the time. She'd been here before without being bothered. Well, not exactly *here.* She'd helped establish a shelter for battered women in this area, and visited it occasionally to make sure things were running well. But it was six blocks away.

Six blocks made a difference. And she hadn't gone there alone.

She'd reached the corner again. The woman standing there gave her a hostile glare. She was an Amazon, six feet tall and stacked. Her hair was long and curly and unnaturally red, and her skimpy top revealed excellent muscle definition in her abs. She did have a coat—red leather, and rather similar to Claudia's, though Claudia's was an electric blue. But it hung open. Her fingernails were the color of dried blood and were long enough to have been registered as weapons.

Claudia thought she must be cold. ''Hello,'' she said brightly. ''Chilly out, isn't it? At least the wind isn't blowing.''

The woman expressed a desire for Claudia to leave. She used very direct language. Claudia's grandmother would have washed her mouth out with soap.

''Look,'' Claudia said, ''I'm not trying to make trouble. I'm just nervous. Those guys in the middle of the block are giving me a hard time.''

She snorted. ''Maybe you're not so dumb as you look.''

''Probably not.'' Claudia kept smiling. ''I like your boots.''

The woman's gaze flickered down to her cowboy boots. They were red and purple. She looked up again, suspicious. ''Somethin' tells me they ain't your usual style.''

''Well,'' Claudia said judiciously, ''the skirt wouldn't work for me.'' Purple leather ending a finger's width below the crotch—no, Claudia couldn't quite picture herself in that. ''But I could go for a pair of boots like that, especially if they came in a blue that went with my coat. Did you buy them someplace I'd be scared to go?''

The woman made a rusty sound. After a second Claudia realized it was a chuckle. ''Probably. Look, chickie, what you doin' here, anyway? You ain't lookin' for business.''

''I'm waiting for a man.''

She sighed. ''Ain't we all.''

Claudia nodded philosophically. ''This particular man went in that brown building two doors down about twenty minutes ago. I was going to follow him, but...it didn't seem like a good idea.'' A single glance inside had persuaded her of that. She had no idea which floor he was on, much less which room, and the hallway was not a good place to wait. It was dark, dirty and stank of things she preferred not to think about. Bad as the street was, it was an improvement over waiting for Ethan inside that building.

At first she'd waited by his car, but not for long. Two men had started across the street toward her. She'd glanced at her watch, tapped her foot, then set off down the street as if she were late for an appointment.

She'd been walking up and down the block ever since.

A car honked as it approached the corner. Claudia's temporary companion thrust out a hip and drew one hand up her body provocatively. The driver looked, but his gaze flicked to Claudia. He shook his head and drove on.

"Look, you're cuttin' into my trade," the woman said impatiently. "Go be nervous someplace else."

"Why did he look at me and change his mind?" Claudia said, vaguely offended. She glanced down at her charcoal-gray slacks, which she'd worn with a red sweater that didn't show beneath her electric-blue leather coat. "I suppose I'm dressed wrong."

The woman made that rusty noise again. "Honey, you are *all* wrong. He probably thought you were a cop."

"A cop?" She grinned, tickled by the idea. "That's never happened before."

"Now, me, I think you look more like one o' those rich bitch do-gooders that runs that place over on Meadow."

"Is that bad?"

She shrugged. "S'pose someone needs to see to those poor cows that lets their men beat on 'em. What you ought to do," she said, fixing Claudia with a firm frown, "is get 'em to a gym, get 'em strong enough to hit back. *I* don't have no trouble with my man messin' with me that way."

"I'll bet you don't." Claudia gave a judicious nod. "But a lot of those women are beat up on the inside, too. Even if they were strong enough physically to fight back, they don't have any fight up here like you do.'' Claudia tapped the side of her head. ''You can tell people something all day, but until they have it inside them, it doesn't do any good.''

''Guess you really ain't as dumb as you look,'' the other woman said grudgingly. Then some radar had her head swiveling. Another car was slowing. She strutted up to the curb, tossed back her coat and did that hip-jut thing again, running her hand up her body.

Claudia thought of what she'd just said. She could talk all day about self-respect and the price this woman paid for using her body as merchandise. She could talk about options and programs that might help her retrain for another profession. And none of it would mean a thing, not unless there was a voice inside the woman whispering some of the same things. No one could afford to hope until they believed change was possible.

This time the car pulled up to the curb. The passenger window slid down and the woman bent over to speak through it, tossing back that long, curly hair. She laughed low in her throat. It sounded nothing like the rusty chuckle Claudia had heard earlier.

The driver reached across the seat and opened the door. The woman started to get in—and paused, glancing over her shoulder. ''You stay away from that Hector. He gets high, he gets stupid. And mean. Likes to cut on women.''

''Wait,'' Claudia said, moving forward. ''Who's Hector?''

''And don' be standing on my spot. My man come around, he ain't gonna like it. He got a strong sense of territory.'' She slammed the door.

''But which one is...''

The car pulled away.

"Hector," Claudia finished in a whisper.

A drop of water plunked on her cheek. Another struck the back of her hand. She looked up. "Oh, hell." Rain. That was all she needed.

Time to get out of here. No cabs were going to come cruising by, so that meant hoofing it. The shelter was six blocks to the west...she thought. Claudia tapped her toe and tried to remember the route the cab had taken. They'd passed a fast-food place a few blocks back, but how many? Three, she thought. That would make it closer than the shelter.

Two more drops hit her head. Big, fat, cold raindrops.

She started walking quickly back down the street. Maybe the hecklers in the doorway would go inside. Surely even rough, tough gang members didn't stand around in the rain when they could go inside and be dry. It had smelled awful inside the building that had swallowed Ethan, though. A little rain might not seem so bad compared to breathing that muck.

Apparently it didn't. The three loungers didn't go inside. No, they'd been joined by a fourth.

Ethan's building was just ahead. Should she go in it? Cross the street? She simply could not make herself believe she'd be safer inside that building. They could corner her in there.

Cross the street, then. Claudia turned sharply and edged between two parked cars. More drops fell. It wasn't quite raining yet, but it was working its way up to it.

She didn't see anyone on the other side of the

street. Yes, this was better. She'd just wait for the next two cars to go by and—

Three young men flowed into her path, coming from both sides. Two were black, one white, but otherwise they looked identical in their baggy pants and tight T-shirts and red-and-black jackets. The one in the middle smiled. His teeth were large and crooked. "Hey, babe. Goin' somewhere?"

She backed up carefully and pulled the pepper spray from her purse.

Two big hands closed around her arms from behind. "Gotcha," a fourth man said cheerfully from far too close. He giggled when she tried to jerk away, and pulled her backward.

Off balance, she fell up against him. He smelled sour and she couldn't aim her pepper spray. "Let go of me."

"Hey, that's not friendly. You don' want us to think you ain't friendly."

"Why would I care?" She tried again to pull free. His fingers dug in harder. It hurt. "Let go, dammit."

He gave her a little shake. "Hector, she don't care."

The others had formed up around them. One of them shook his head. "Hector gets his feelings hurt when people aren't friendly."

"You don't wanna hurt Hector's feelings, do you?"

That brought a round of snickers.

"Hey, what's that you got, sugar?"

One of them laughed. "In her hand, jerk-face," the first one said amiably. "I know what she's got between her legs.'' He snatched the pepper spray away from her. ''Why, that is real unfriendly.''

Claudia had always thought that the saying about your heart leaping into your throat was just an expression. But there hers was, nearly choking her while it pounded away in the wrong spot.

''You boys are scarin' the poor thing,'' the one in the middle said. He was nineteen or twenty years old and as pale as Claudia. His long, stringy hair was the color of used dishwater. His eyes looked funny—the pupils weren't right. ''See, we just wanted to ask you somethin', sugar. We been havin' a discussion. Jarmon here says the only reason a rich white bitch like you visits our turf is to get herself some dark meat. Now, me, I say maybe you want some, maybe you don't. But Jarmon, he do have a point. Why else you be here?''

They were grinning, happy with a chance to ease their boredom. The rain had worked its way up to a heavy drizzle. It didn't seem to bother them.

She swallowed, trying to make her heart go back down where it belonged. ''Are—are you Hector?'' Oh, she didn't like the way her voice shook. Or the way the dirty person behind her was rubbing one hand up and down her arm.

''You know me?'' He made an astonished face. ''Hey, boys, she knows me! Maybe I'm famous, huh?'' He moved closer, smiling widely. ''Maybe you came here to see me, huh?''

''I never date men who pull the wings off flies for fun.''

That brought a round of laughter and some comments about the sort of things Hector did for entertainment. She shivered and told herself it was the cold water falling on her bare head that caused it. The fat drops were falling faster.

"Hey, Felipe, you bein' greedy. We need to let the lady choose."

"Yeah, that's only polite. Let her pick."

"Here go, then, Jarmon. Catch!" The one holding her shoved her at one of the others. Who laughed and shoved her at the next one. Who spun her around, squeezed her breast and passed her to another.

She stomped on someone's foot and was spun around hard again, nearly falling. Her purse slipped from her shoulder and she swung it at someone. He grabbed it, threw it on the ground and flung her at the next one. She tried to punch him, missed and was spun to the next set of grasping hands—and the next. Faster and faster, they shoved her around in dizzy circles. She was terrified, cold, wet and furious. And helpless.

Oh God, dear God, please make them stop. Because *she* couldn't.

Until a low voice growled, "Let go of her."

The hands withdrew. She stopped moving. The world swung lazily around her once, twice, like a saucer rocking on its rim. Then settled.

Ethan stood six feet away. His legs were spread wide. He wore a black hat with silver conches circling the crown and a wide, flat brim, and he carried a black walking stick, wet and shiny from the rain. His trench coat was long and black and none too clean, and he looked huge. Wonderfully, fabulously *big*.

Also angry.

''Hey, man,'' one of them said. ''We was just playin'. No one's hurt.''

''Come here, Claudia.''

Oh, yes. Good idea. She took a wobbly step toward him—and Hector's arm shot out and wrapped around her waist, hauling her up against him. He laughed. ''Sorry, big man. Get your own woman. We found this one first.''

''Wrong. She's mine. You need to let go of her. Now.''

Claudia's street-corner friend had been right. When Hector got high, he got stupid. He laughed again. ''I don' think so. You're big, but there's one of you and there's, let's see—one, two, three, four of us. Yep, four. An' I say we got dibs.''

Things happened *very* fast then.

Ethan's stick shot out and tapped Hector on the head. He made a funny noise and let go of her, and this time she didn't hesitate—she shot straight for Ethan. But one of them grabbed her arm, spinning her around, and dammit! She'd had enough of being spun! She tried to knee him in the groin and connected with *something,* but the other two were going at Ethan real fast and one had a knife. Someone screamed.

Ethan's stick was everywhere. *Thunk, crack, whap!* A knee, a hand, someone's ribs—the knife went flying, so she stopped screaming, jerked herself free and got out of the way.

Only it was all over. Three of them were on the ground—two sitting, one flat out. That was Hector. His eyes were closed and there was blood on his head, mixing with the rain. Another one was cursing Ethan and clutching his thigh. He seemed to think his leg was broken. The fourth one was backing up, his hands held out, palms up. "I didn't pull steel on you, okay? Didn't hurt her none, either. No harm done, okay?"

Ethan made a noise low in his throat. It didn't sound like agreement.

Claudia gulped, cleared her throat and said, "I would *really* like to leave now."

"Get your purse."

She edged around the one clutching his leg and snatched her bag from the ground.

Ethan was holding out his keys. His eyes never left her assailants. "Open the driver's side and climb in."

She ran to his car and did that. Her hands were shaking, so it took her a moment to get the key in the lock. Once inside, she stuck the key in the ignition, tossed her purse on the floorboard and scooted over.

Ethan was right behind her. "Duck," he said, and she did, and his stick went over her head and into the back seat as he slid behind the wheel. The door slammed shut.

One of them had gotten back on his feet. He was holding his side with one hand and a knife with the other, and he and the one that had been left standing were coming toward the car. Hector was still on the ground, as was the one whose leg might be broken.

Two more young men in red-and-black jackets came running out of the doorway the others had been lounging around.

Ethan gunned the car backward a couple of feet, jerked the steering wheel, shifted and pulled out from between the parked cars. He missed the one in front by nearly an inch.

Claudia let out her breath. Oh, my. She didn't feel well at all. ''That was,'' she began, ''you and your stick, I mean...I've never seen anything like that.''

''Claudia. Shut up.''

She bristled and looked at him—took a *good* look at him—and saw the white-knuckled hands gripping the steering wheel, the white look around his eyes, and the thin, grim slash of his mouth.

Out of the frying pan, she thought. And remembered what Rick had told her about what happened years ago, when Ethan lost his temper back in high school. Guilt struck.

She shut up.

Eight

There was a buzzing in his ears. Ethan gripped the steering wheel as hard as he could. If he held on tightly enough, maybe the shaking inside him wouldn't get out.

He hadn't been this angry since he was sixteen. Or this scared, though back then the fear had hit after the fight, not before. When he was waiting to see if Robert Parkington would make it through surgery. Waiting to find out if he would be arrested. If he was a killer.

Trying to put that out of his mind was like trying not to think of a particular word. The images were just there. And the feelings.

He remembered the way Parkington's head had sounded when it hit the railing. A dull sort of crack, but loud. The second he'd heard that he'd known things had gone wrong. Bad-wrong, more wrong than anything since the day his aunt told him about his parents and the mugger his father had tried to fight off.

One of Robert's buddies had swung at Ethan, still pissed and not realizing how wrong things were. Ethan had thrown him aside. Just picked him up and tossed him, and that shouldn't have been possible. The guy had to have weighed one-seventy, and while Ethan had been young and strong, he was no Superman.

But he'd had to get to Robert Parkington, who'd been lying so still, crumpled up against the iron railing. Lying where Ethan's blow had sent him, a blow struck in the heat of rage, with all his strength.

Parkington had been a bully and a coward, but he hadn't seriously hurt anyone. He hadn't deserved to come so near to dying. He wasn't a killer. Not like the pair of muggers who'd killed Ethan's parents. Or the lowlifes who'd been tormenting Claudia today.

This time he hadn't lost control. But it had been close. From one breath to the next he hadn't been sure he could hang on. *Use your temper, don't lose it.* That was what his *sensei* had told him later. Anger was a force, like electricity or gravity. Properly channeled, it could be used. Uncontrolled, it destroyed.

He'd done okay today. He'd stayed loose, let the anger flow through him instead of letting it direct him. He'd done the amount of damage he'd had to do to get Claudia safely away, and no more. But when he thought of her white face, the wild fear in her eyes, the way she'd tried to fight back… Damn them. Pathetic, miserable excuses for men, tossing Claudia around their circle like kids tormenting a kitten. He wanted to go back and hit them again. And again.

And when he thought of what would have happened to her if he hadn't come along... "Dammit, why don't you say something?"

"You told me to shut up."

"Since when do you do what you're told?" Helluva a time for her to discover a talent for obedience. He needed her to talk, to say stupid things and argue with him so he could yell at her.

"Could you put the heater on? I'm rather chilly."

For the first time since getting in the car, he looked at her. She was sitting cross-legged, her arms hugged around her, her hair plastered to her cheeks and hanging down her back in sodden strings.

Not only was he violent, he was stupid, too. He might have enough adrenaline churning up his system to keep him warm for another year or two. She didn't. She was scared, cold and in shock.

He switched the heater on. "Are you okay?" he asked gruffly. "Hurt anywhere?"

"No. Oh, some bumps and bruises, but nothing important. I'm a little shaken up." She held out her hands, studied them a moment as if checking out what the shakes looked like, then dropped them with a sigh. "I'm so sorry, Ethan. I was an idiot."

She'd taken the words right out of his mouth.

"This must be upsetting for you. Rick told me about what happened when you were in high school."

"Son of a bitch!"

"But what happened today wasn't the same at all," she told him earnestly. "Not that you were truly in the wrong then. The police did rule it was self-defense. They *jumped* you, for heaven's sake. Three of them, one of you. Which must make it seem similar, but—''

''Did Rick tell you that Robert Parkington could have died?'' he asked savagely. ''That I broke his jaw and sent him crashing headfirst into an iron fence, and he ended up with a depressed skull fracture?''

''Yes, he told me. You must have been terrified.''

She just didn't get it. ''I saw red. I was in a rage, not a terrified funk.''

''Well, anger is just fear turned outward, isn't it? Fear points in, anger points out.''

''You don't know what you're talking about.'' His mouth was dry, the way it had been when they'd grabbed his arms and pinned them behind his back. He'd been so surprised. Stupidly surprised. It hadn't occurred to him that a bunch of frat brats would pull something like that.

''I know some people say that fear leads to anger, but I think anger is just fear turned inside out.''

With Ethan held by his two buddies, Parkington had hit him. A blow in the stomach first. It had hurt, but mostly made him mad. His abs had been rock solid from all those sit-ups the coach insisted on. So he'd spat in Parkington's face, called him a coward. Parkington had flushed an ugly red and hit Ethan in the face then, using both fists, one after the other. His jaw. His eye. His cheek. He still had a scar there.

And Ethan had come unglued.

Claudia didn't seem the least fazed by his lack of response. ''Rick said they'd been picking on someone you knew. I gather the boy was rather undersized, unable to defend himself. You made them stop.''

"Three college boys show up at a high school hangout, it figures they're looking for trouble. Someone to push around. I decided they ought to get what they wanted—only with someone who could push back." He shook his head. "Talk about stupid."

"Standing up for him wasn't stupid. The way you went about it wasn't too bright, maybe."

He snorted. "You can say that again." He'd invited all three of them outside, figuring he'd find a buddy or two hanging around out back if he needed backup. Not much caring if he didn't, though. He was big, he knew how to handle himself and he wasn't drunk the way they were. "I thought I was hot stuff. And I liked to fight."

"I can't say I understand *that,* but a lot of adolescent males do seem to enjoy punching one another. You don't like to fight anymore. Though you *are* very good at it." There was a hint of a lift at the end of her sentence, leaving it dangling halfway between statement and question.

Ethan frowned. What he felt was more complicated than liking or not liking. "About two months after Parkington was released from the hospital, I found out he was in physical therapy. He'd lost partial function in his left arm, something to do with the pressure on his brain from the skull fracture. I was…upset. My uncle talked me into taking judo lessons."

"That seems like an odd way to deal with your feelings."

"It was exactly what I needed. Uncle Luke pointed out that I couldn't trade in my body for a weaker version, and I couldn't guarantee I'd never have to defend myself or someone else, so I'd better learn how to do it without killing anyone.''

''Oh.'' She thought that over for a moment, then nodded. ''Is that where you learned to fight with a stick?''

''Eventually. First I had to learn discipline.'' How to fight cool, not hot. How to avoid fights when he could, and how to win one as quickly as possible if he couldn't avoid it, using as much force as necessary. And no more.

How to trust himself again.

''I think I'd like your uncle. Um...'' She sneaked a glance at him. ''Did Parkington regain use of his arm?''

''Yeah. Pretty much.'' After Ethan started working part-time for his uncle Thomas and had learned something about the detective business, he'd undertaken some private surveillance. From what he'd been able to tell, Parkington used the arm normally.

''I'm glad.''

She didn't say anything more. After a few minutes Ethan frowned.

What had just happened here?

His hands were easy on the steering wheel. The tight band across his shoulders had loosened, and that deep-down shaking was gone. There was a funny feeling in his gut, sort of a visceral humming. Not unpleasant. In fact, he felt...good. Energized.

Of course, below his gut could be found the most likely reason for his sense of well-being. Nothing like a little arousal to make a man feel alive. It was a perfectly natural reaction, he assured himself. Given the adrenaline cocktail he'd served his body, it would be amazing if he weren't somewhat aroused.

But his anger was gone. Kaput. Vanished. Dammit, he'd wanted to be mad. Mad was better than thinking about what could have happened to her. By God, she deserved for him to be angry.

So how come he'd been discussing the worst time in his life with her?

Obviously, she'd mounted a sneak attack. Caught him off guard. That wouldn't happen again. Just as well he'd calmed down, though. He still intended to read her the riot act, but now he could do so coolly. Rationally. When he was through, she'd never even think about pulling a stunt like this again.

Not that he meant to be too harsh. She'd had a rough time, he thought, glancing at her. She wasn't hugging herself for warmth anymore, but she sure didn't look like the polished Ms. Barone. Her face was still pale and her hair straggled down in those wet rattails.

They'd nearly reached her apartment. "I'm going in with you," he announced.

"Oh," she said, smiling brightly, "that won't be necessary."

"I find it extremely necessary." Calm, cool and reasonable. That was how he'd handle this, he thought as he pulled up right in front of her building and killed the engine. He opened his door.

She grabbed his arm. "You don't want to get out here."

"Don't waste your breath arguing."

"This is a tow-away zone."

"So?" He slammed the door shut behind him.

Nine

Claudia's insides were jumping like popcorn. Or like bacon frying—sizzle, pop, splat! Hot-grease attack, stinging on the inside of her skin. Her eyes were dry and hot. So why did she think that any second she might start crying?

She needed to be alone. Badly. And the stupid man who had rescued her insisted on riding up in the elevator with her, looking like a thunderstorm about to happen. She needed him to go away…before she threw herself into his arms and sobbed like a baby.

That image made her cringe inside. So she'd let him get the lecture out of his system. He was obviously bursting with it. Like a boil, she thought as she got her key out. Or a pimple. Pop it, let it drain, and it went away. Ethan would go away soon.

She stuck her key in the door. Look there. Her hand

wasn't shaking anymore. She was going to be just fine.

"All right," she said as she closed her door. "Go ahead and say what you have to. If you hurry, I'll have time for a shower before I have to dress for the board meeting this afternoon. And maybe you can get your car before it's impounded."

"Would you forget about my damned car?" He began pacing, his voice getting louder as he told her what an incredibly stupid thing she'd done. He paused by her white velvet love seat, still talking, and ran a hand over his hair, making it stand up in damp spikes.

That love seat used to be her grandmother's. She'd had it recovered once—white did show every little stain—and had hunted and hunted until she found a fabric that was almost identical to the original. She liked to curl up there and read. Not often, but once in a while she gave herself permission to be utterly useless for a day. Novels only, when she was indulging. Fun books. She especially liked the ones about lords and ladies, or a good fantasy with a dragon and…

And Ethan was standing right in front of her. "Have you heard a word I've said?" he demanded.

"Oh. Well, no, I don't think so. Normally I enjoy a good argument, but I'm really not up to it right now, and while you might be able to bull your way in here, I don't *think* you can make me listen, can you?" She smiled at him brightly.

The strangest thing happened. All that thunder and lightning drained right out of his face. He looked stricken. "Aw, Claudia. Look at you. Just look at you." And he gathered her up in his arms.

He was so large and solid. And damp. His coat was still wet from the rain, and it smelled like cigarette smoke. Her breathing wasn't working right. Things were hitching up inside her. "I'm all right," she told him.

"I know you are." He stroked her hair. "You're fine. I'm so sorry, sugar. Don't smile like that anymore. You don't have to smile like that with me. You're safe. You're okay."

"Y-yes, I am." All by themselves her hands clutched fistfuls of his coat, and she realized the shakes hadn't gone away, after all. They'd just moved, lodging in her spine. One long tremor passed up it. "They wanted to hurt me, Ethan! They didn't even hate me—I was just there, and they were bored, and maybe they've had terrible lives and don't know any better. But it was *me* they had."

"Shh," he said, and ran his big hand along her back, stroking another tremor out the way a squeegee strokes water from a windshield. "Forget them. They don't matter."

"Everyone *matters*. Even them. But I—I—" She gulped.

"I shouldn't have yelled at you. I wasn't going to, but whenever I stopped being mad I got scared all over again. You were right about that anger and fear business. I've never been so scared in my life."

"M-me, neither." And she gave up and cried.

Maybe the ability to cry easily was another feminine skill she lacked. Claudia didn't cry often, but when tears did hit, they hit hard. Ethan didn't say a word. He ran his hand up and down her back, using long, soothing strokes. He didn't tell her to quit crying, or try to fix things so she'd stop. He just held her.

The storm passed as quickly as it had hit. Soon she hung, limp and quiet, in Ethan's arms. She sniffed once. Again.

"Better?" he said in a low, husky voice.

She nodded her head against his shoulder. Such wonderful shoulders. Wonderful arms, wonderful chest…wonderful man. She rubbed her cheek against that hard, comforting shoulder.

"Ah…Claudia?"

"Hmm?" She turned her head without lifting it, and there was his neck. Strong and warm and smelling so good. She nuzzled it.

"You might want to stop doing that."

"Why?" And why was she still gripping his coat? That wonderful chest was *beneath* the smoke-stinky coat. She slid her hands inside the damp trench coat and sighed with pleasure. The cotton of his shirt was warm from his body.

"I'm having a problem here."

"Are you?" She looped her arms around his neck, which brought their bodies firmly together. His body provided intimate evidence of what he meant. "Hmm…no. *Not* a problem."

His hands tightened at her waist. "You're probably impaired right now, just coming off a crying jag and all. Not thinking straight."

"Probably."

"We weren't going to do this."

"I've changed my mind."

"Thank God." The last word came out as a puff

of air against her lips just before his mouth covered hers.

Her eyes closed. She leaned into his kiss and sweetness poured through her, a tactile hum buzzing from lips to throat, groin to thighs to the pockets at the backs of her knees. Her fingertips tingled. The wet rasp of his tongue demanded her attention, but his hands coursed up and down her body, distracting her.

"This coat," he muttered. "It has to go."

"Yours, too. I don't like it." She pulled it off his shoulders. He cooperated, yanking his arms out and letting it fall to the floor.

That was all the cooperation he had in mind, though. He wanted her coat off, and he wanted it off now. And her sweater. And then he unfastened the catch on her bra.

When he pushed it aside he made a funny noise, sort of a delighted grunt. "I've thought about these," he said, cupping her breasts. "Sweet, creamy pears. I need to taste them again."

So he did. Claudia approved of his initiative and told him so silently, clutching his head, running her fingers over his ears, his jaw, where she felt his muscles work as he began to suck.

Oh. *Oh!* Heat melted her knees and made mush of her brain. He knew what to do, though. He scooped her up and placed her on the love seat, with himself on top.

This was much better. He propped himself up on one elbow and rubbed his chest across the tips of her breasts. She leaned up, caught his head and kissed him again, then broke away to run her tongue along the whorls of one ear. Intoxicated by intimacy, she rubbed her hands over his back, down to his butt.

He quivered. And ran one hand down between her legs.

She jolted. Her eyes flew open wide.

Outside, the rain poured down, muting the light in the room to a rainy-day gray. The velvet was plush and warm beneath her back. Ethan's face hovered close to hers, his eyes dark with pleasure and intent on her. In sudden, dizzy splendor she broke with gravity, falling up into his gaze.

And realized she was about to do something irrevocable.

Claudia might have stopped then, frozen by that sense of change, vast and permanent, hovering over her, but he began to knead her in a rhythm that drove thought from her head. She forgot everything except how to feel. And move.

She curled one leg up around his, wanting to grip him with every part of her. That brought him closer, but not close enough. His clothes hampered her, so she tore at the buttons on his shirt.

Claudia had never seen a stampede outside of the movies. She'd certainly never participated in one. But that was what happened next—a mad stampede to strip, unzip, unbutton, both of them frenzied for skin. Yet skin wasn't enough. Or else it was too much, sending them scrambling for union before they'd removed everything properly.

The love seat was cramped, especially for a man Ethan's size. He dealt with that by lifting her left leg and placing it along the back of the love seat. Then he put her right leg on his shoulder, leaving her utterly exposed. And excited. He groaned as he sank into her.

She gasped and dug her fingers into his back. “There is rather a lot of you, Ethan.”

“And you are perfect.” He licked her bottom lip. His hips shifted. “Hot and slick and perfect.”

He thrust slowly once, then again. But she’d been at a high pitch before he came inside her. Lingering was unbearable now. For him, too, it seemed. His control cracked on the third thrust, and he began pounding into her.

Friction and sweat-slick skin. The slap of flesh against flesh. The musky scent of sex, and a delirious pressure that built and built. She cried out, telling him to hold her, to touch her—and he slipped a hand between their bodies. He touched her exactly where she needed.

The world exploded. A few thrusts later, he followed her over the edge.

There wasn’t room for him to collapse fully. Her leg slipped from his shoulder. He sagged onto his elbows. Little aftershocks pinged through her body, a visceral version of the afterimages left by a flashbulb. She smiled sleepily, smugly, and drifted her hand over the wrinkled cotton still covering his shoulder. “Mmm.”

His chest was heaving like a bellows. “Yeah.” He lifted his head and smiled down at her, and he looked so disheveled and happy that the single word was quite satisfactory.

A sound from the front of the room took a second to penetrate her hazy brain, and a second longer to be processed.

It was the sound of her door being opened. And it was accompanied by Stacy's voice. "Claudia? You home? I came to visit my cold cuts. You'll never guess what— *Ark!*"

The door slammed shut again.

Claudia stared up at Ethan. And began, helplessly, to giggle at the expression on his face. "Oh," she gasped, "oh, my. You've never met Stacy, have you?"

"I still haven't," he snapped. There was an embarrassed flush high on his cheekbones. He sat up and reached for his jeans and underwear, muttering, "Cold cuts. She wants to visit her cold cuts." He paused to fix Claudia with an accusing stare. "And this person has a *key* to your apartment?"

That sent her into whoops. "I'm sorry. I shouldn't laugh. If it had been anyone except Stacy…she couldn't have seen much, Ethan, she was gone so fast. But, oh, if you could have *seen* the look on your face!"

His grin was small and reluctant, but there. "I guess it could have been worse. Does anyone else have a key they're likely to use? Like, say, your mother or father?"

"Now, *that* would not be funny." Absently Claudia reached for the dangling ends of her bra and fastened it, then looked around for her panties.

They were decorating the Tiffany floor lamp. She retrieved them and stood to pull them on. "Stacy lives across the hall. She's my best friend, so of course she has a key. Though normally she doesn't use it to visit her c-cold cuts." A giggle snuck out, but she restrained herself. ''Her refrigerator went out yesterday, you see. She came over last night—''

Last night. ''Oh, God,'' Claudia moaned, closing her eyes. ''Neil.''

''The boyfriend.'' Ethan's lip curled. He jammed one foot into the leg of his jeans. ''I guess you had another attack of amnesia. Pretty convenient memory you have.''

She flushed, guilty and mortified. ''Don't you sneer at me.''

''You going to tell your lover about us?''

''I— Neil isn't—oh, if you're going to be hateful you can just leave!''

''Fine.'' He yanked up the zipper on his jeans. ''Great.'' He grabbed his trench coat off the floor, shrugged it on and took a step toward the door. Then stopped and heaved a great sigh. ''No, it isn't fine.''

He turned back to her. ''I forgot about the boyfriend, too. About everything except having you. The thing is...'' He grimaced and scrubbed his hair back, making it even more of a mess. ''I don't poach on another man's territory. And I sure as hell don't share.''

Claudia felt like a pinball machine—lights flashing, emotions bouncing around all over the place. ''We aren't lovers, and I am *not* territory.''

''The hell we aren't!'' He crossed to her in two swift strides, seized her face in both hands and kissed her. He made a thorough job of it, and when he raised his head her insides were jumbled worse than before.

''Tell me again we aren't lovers,'' he demanded.

Claudia drifted back, blinking. ''Um...I meant that Neil and I aren't lovers.''

"Oh." A grin broke out on his face. "That's all right, then. You'll tell him you can't see him anymore. Because right now. you and I definitely are lovers."

Her heart gave a little skip. "At the moment, you mean. Temporarily."

"Yes." His voice softened and his eyes looked worried. "I'm not looking for anything long-term, Claudia. I should have said so before."

"You didn't have a chance, did you? I swept you off your feet."

"So you did." His smile returned. "'Practically perfect in every way', that's you. Who would have thought I'd have a hot affair with Mary Poppins?"

"Mary Poppins?" she exclaimed indignantly.

"Sure. She was always fixing things for other people, too." He dropped a kiss on her nose. "If you hurry, you can still get that shower before you have to go to your meeting."

"And maybe your car is still downstairs. Though I doubt it."

"Maybe," he said cheerfully. He was humming Tchaikovsky's *1812 Overture* as he closed her door behind him.

It took Claudia's pinballing brain a moment to catch up with the significance of that. The *Overture* was a triumphant paean to Napolean's defeat at Waterloo. Just who, she wondered, did Ethan think had triumphed today—and who had met their Waterloo?

She fell back on the couch, laughing.

Ethan beat the wrecker to his car by mere moments. The truck had been stuck in traffic, he learned.

Once in a while, fate smiled. For the rest of the afternoon he found himself smiling back. Humming at odd moments. Even the lack of progress in the case didn't have the power to depress his spirits. Boots's tip turned out to be worthless, though it took Ethan all afternoon to confirm that the Norblusky his stoolie told him about wasn't the Norblusky Ethan needed to find. He couldn't get worked up about the wasted time, though. For someone who'd done something he'd been convinced would be a major mistake, he sure felt good.

Late that afternoon he looked up his uncle Thomas. Aunt Adele directed him to the detached garage out back, which didn't surprise him. The main reason Thomas Mallory had retired was so he could devote more time to his hobby. Ethan could hear motors whirring before he reached the side door of the garage. He opened it, and there stood his uncle in the middle of his kingdom.

Four tables covered with miniature roads, cars, trees and buildings encircled him. A little locomotive was huffing up the papier-mâché hill at the far end, burping tiny puffs of smoke from its miniature smokestack. Ethan grinned. "You've been changing things around again. The feedstore's new, isn't it?"

"Got it last week." Thomas adjusted the speed of the locomotive and it slowed to a halt. He was a tall, narrow man, slightly stooped, with wispy gray hair beneath a red baseball cap. His reading glasses always looked in danger of slipping off the end of his long, narrow nose. "What else do you see that's changed?"

Ethan groaned, but more from habit than real irritation. Uncle Thomas was forever cross-examining him. It was a holdover from when he'd trained Ethan. ''Detection is fifty percent observation, fifty percent perspiration,'' his uncle used to say.

Thomas waited, his eyes patient and amused. He liked to claim the prerogative of age when Ethan complained about his little pop quizzes. ''Makes me feel useful,'' he'd say, trying to look pathetic. He actually did pathetic pretty well. Or grandfatherly, or helpless, innocuous, friendly, upset. The outraged consumer was one of his best bits. He could be whatever the subject he was questioning needed him to be.

Uncle Thomas had never had much of a head for business, but he was hell on wheels at getting people to talk.

''Manipulative old bastard,'' Ethan muttered.

''Show some respect, boy.'' Uncle Thomas's eyes twinkled. ''What would your aunt Adele say if she heard that kind of language?''

''That I shouldn't listen in on her private conversations,'' Ethan retorted. ''Since that's what she calls you when she's mad at you.'' But he capitulated, as they'd both known he would. ''Okay, okay. The feedstore is new, like I said. The wagon by the feedstore, too. The store next to the bank has changed—used to be a drugstore, didn't it? And something's different about the mayor's house.'' He studied it a moment. ''I've got it. The oak tree with the little swing is gone.''

''Blasted cat of Adele's got hold of it. Why that fur ball wants to chew on fake trees, I'll never know.'' Thomas Mallory ducked under the table that held up the east end of his domain, straightening with a grunt. He shoved his glasses up a split second before they fell off. "Not bad. Guess you have learned a little something about observation. But you didn't come here in the middle of a workday to…uh-oh." He stopped, frowning.

"What?" Ethan looked around, but couldn't see anything wrong.

"You got laid."

Ethan felt his cheeks heating. "Come on, Nero Wolfe. You can't tell just by looking at me."

"Sure I can. Haven't seen you this relaxed in months. Either you've been laid, or you're in love."

Ethan's mouth went dry. His uncle was just trying to get a rise out of him. He refused to jump to the bait, but for some reason he couldn't think of a thing to say.

Thomas carefully unhitched the locomotive and inspected it, tipping his head back to look through his half glasses. "Think the smoke was getting a little thin…yep, the reservoir's dry." He picked up a funnel and a water pitcher. "I hope it wasn't that Cecily Barone who put a smile on your face."

"Claudia. Her name is Claudia, and what do you know about her, anyway?"

"Rick mentioned her."

Ethan's mellow mood was evaporating fast. "Rick's got a big mouth."

"Guess it's a sensitive subject, seeing how much she's like Bianca."

"Claudia is nothing like Bianca."

"Oh?" Thomas layered a wealth of disbelief into that single syllable. "She's rich. She's blond. And her family doesn't like you."

"Why is everyone so fascinated by hair color?"

Ethan jammed his hands in his pockets. "You have no idea if her family likes me or not. Hell, neither do I. They don't know me."

"You're investigating them, aren't you? Stands to reason."

Especially if he ended up finding evidence that put her brother behind bars. "Look, what's between me and Claudia is just that—between me and Claudia. I didn't come here for advice on my love life."

"I suppose not." Thomas put the locomotive back on the tracks. "Must be work, then."

"I've got a job for you."

"Oh?" Uncle Thomas straightened slightly. "Well, I don't know...I'm pretty busy around here."

This was another of their little routines. Now and then Ethan had a task that was particularly suited to his uncle's abilities. Thomas always pretended he wasn't interested, but in truth he loved being asked and enjoyed keeping his hand in. "I need a confused old man who people will bend a few rules to help out."

Thomas chuckled. "Nothing like some gray hairs to make folks think you're harmless, and senility covers a multitude of sins. What do you need this poor old man to find out?"

"I need to find a man named Norblusky. Rick talked to his sister yesterday. He's convinced she knows where her brother is hiding, but he couldn't get a thing out of her."

Thomas settled down on the tall stool by his workbench, smiling with satisfaction. "Rick's good, but he carries that mantle of cop around with him. People don't like talking to cops. Tell me about it—why you need this Norblusky, what his sister is like, why the man's hiding out.''

It was a great relief to do just that, much better than discussing his relationship with Claudia. Ethan paced as he briefed his uncle. Then the two of them brainstormed about the best approach to take with Norblusky's sister, who would be doubly on her guard now.

''Rick didn't think there was much love lost between Norblusky and his sister?'' Thomas asked.

Ethan shook his head. ''She was wary and close-mouthed, but he had the feeling she was protecting herself more than her brother.''

''Don't think you need me, then.'' Thomas sighed and rubbed his hands on his thighs. ''Follow the money, son. If she's protecting her own interests, chances are there's money involved. Dig up her social security number and whatever else you can find, and have Ernie check out her bank account.''

Ernie was the I.B. Ethan used. He shifted, uncomfortable with what he had to say next. ''You think you could handle that? It isn't as much fun as doing an interview, but...''

His uncle's eyebrows went up. ''You too busy romancing the Barone girl to dig through files?''

''She'll follow me. Claudia, I mean.'' Ethan scowled. ''If I told you what almost happened today...never mind. She's sort of involved in the investigation.''

''The sister of one of your suspects is involved in your investigation?'' Thomas's eyebrows climbed higher. ''Rick said something about that, but I thought he must have it wrong.''

Ethan didn't know how to explain. Thomas hadn't met Claudia. He didn't realize how impossible it would be to shut her out, or what she was really like. Flamboyant in her own way, yeah, but her way wasn't like Bianca's. With Bianca, everything had always been about her. Not Claudia. Her passions revolved around fixing things for others. Helping whoever needed it.

A smile snuck out. Not *all* her passions.

Thomas muttered something under his breath. "All right, all right. I'll help you out. Looks like you're going to need it, with your brain only hitting on two cylinders."

Ethan didn't ask his uncle to explain that comment. He was pretty sure he knew what it meant. They discussed the case a little more, then Thomas asked, "You going to that party your aunt Sophia is giving the twins on Saturday?"

"I don't know. Probably." One of his cousins had twin daughters who would be one year old this weekend. Ethan didn't try to go to every family shindig that came along—in a family the size of his, someone was always having a birthday or an anniversary or something. But the first birthday…well, that was kind of special. And the twins were cute as could be.

"I've got to buy presents for them," he said. "Any suggestions?"

Thomas waved that aside. "Ask your aunt. That's her department. I was thinking you might bring Claudia with you, let us meet her. Unless this is one of your easy-on, easy-over affairs?" He looked at Ethan over the tops of his glasses.

"You're pushing." Was he supposed to make it

look as if Claudia didn't matter? Or subject her to a family party complete with screaming kids, Uncle Harold and other hazards?

"I expect you're right not to ask her. She wouldn't fit in."

Ethan shook his head. "I'm not fifteen anymore. That negative psychology bit won't work."

So how was it, he asked himself as he climbed into his car thirty minutes later, that he'd agreed to invite Claudia to the twins' birthday? *Manipulative old bastard,* he thought with equal parts irritation and affection, and slammed the car door shut.

Ten

"Need any help?" Claudia asked as she entered the kitchen that Saturday.

Stacy was rummaging in Claudia's freezer. Her new refrigerator had been delivered at last, and she was relocating her perishables. "No, you managed to take long enough on the phone that I'm about done."

"My timing's always been good." She set her purse on the table and began digging through it.

Stacy straightened, holding up a foil-wrapped mystery package. "Is this yours or mine?"

"Must be yours. I label mine."

"You would. 'Dia? What's wrong?"

"Oh, nothing."

"Claudia."

She shrugged. "Nothing major. That was Emily on the phone. Seems there's a big family meeting tonight at Uncle Carlo's house.'' And she had an idea for how to make use of that, if she could just find her address book.

''Something's wrong with someone in your family?''

''Not exactly. Derrick claims he has something important to reveal about the arson investigation.''

''And he didn't tell you about it.''

She shook her head.

''Don't take it to heart,'' Stacy said kindly. ''You know what he's like. He wants to one-up you, that's all. Easier to do that if you aren't around.''

''I suppose.'' But it bothered Claudia. Derrick could be a real pain sometimes, turning everything into a competition. The sad truth was that she didn't really enjoy him anymore. She used to. Derrick had been a good big brother when they were kids. He'd taught her how to play poker, ride a bike, use a computer. Maybe, she thought sadly, the problem was that there wasn't anything for him to teach her anymore.

No address book yet, but she found the lipstick she'd been looking for earlier. She twirled it up to make sure it was the right shade.

''Derrick is probably still mad because the family put you in charge of keeping track of Ethan.'' Stacy frowned. ''Not that I'm sure that was such a great idea.''

''Why not?'' Claudia dropped the lipstick back in her purse. No point in applying it now—Ethan would just kiss it off her when he arrived. He was taking her to a party at his aunt's this afternoon. She smiled.

''Throwing you and Ethan together may not have

been such a great idea, that's all. The two of you are doing all kinds of things together these days.''

Claudia snickered. ''You ought to know.''

''I mean—oh, you know what I mean.''

Claudia found it quite amusing that Stacy was more embarrassed than she was about her accidental intrusion last Monday. It wasn't as if she and Ethan had actually been doing anything when Stacy walked in. ''Ethan does have a marvelous bottom, doesn't he?''

''I didn't notice,'' Stacy said stiffly. ''I suppose I was referring to sex, but other things, too. You two are spending pretty much every minute together.''

''Not every minute. He does have other cases he has to spend some time on.'' The first time he'd told her he had to work on a different case, she'd followed him, suspecting trickery. Then felt guilty when it became obvious he'd told the truth. ''But as much as possible, yes. Might as well make the most of it while it lasts. Oh, there it is!'' She pulled out her address book.

''I'm worried about you.''

''About me?'' Claudia was surprised, and somewhat distracted. Where had she left her cell phone? It wasn't on the charger.

''You're not acting like yourself. There's the way you started an affair with Ethan before you broke off with Neil. That's not like you.''

She did feel rotten about that. ''That was a mistake. Neil took it very well when I spoke to him, though.'' Almost too well. A touch of angst over their breakup would have been nice.

''You skipped a Junior League meeting.''

''You know Ethan and I were chasing down a lead

in South Boston that day. I did make sure Mary had my report.''

''And you're forgetting things. That is so not like you.''

Forgetting…oh. Suddenly Claudia understood. ''Oh, dear.'' She dropped the address book and hurried over to hug Stacy. ''I still can't believe I forgot our lunch. You're right—that isn't like me. At least I hope it isn't. I don't want to be the kind of woman who ignores her friends whenever she's involved with a man.''

Stacy flushed. ''You're not.''

''Well, anyway…'' Claudia gave Stacy's shoulders a last squeeze. ''I am sorry. You know how important you are to me, don't you?''

Stacy blinked rapidly, looked down, then had to push her glasses up when they threatened to fall off her little dot of a nose. ''I did get my feelings hurt, I guess,'' she said gruffly.

''I've been distracted lately. And not just by Ethan.''

Though when she thought about last night at his apartment, when she'd knelt in front of him to put the condom on, and— *Not now,* she told herself firmly. Stacy's myopic eyes could zero in on her emotions with uncanny ease. ''Did I mention that Ethan is redoing his place? He has this old brownstone in South Boston, and it's really great. Or will be when he's finished. Who would have thought the man had good taste?'' She shook her head, thinking of his clothes. ''With house stuff, anyway. He's going for a period look. Right now he rents out two of the floors, and—''

"And you're avoiding the subject. I don't think you're distracted, I think you're worried and have worked up a serious case of denial. Is it Ethan?"

She sighed. "Derrick, mostly. I can't put my finger on what's wrong, but something is."

"There's always something wrong in Derrick's life."

"I know, but…something's different. I've always thought of him as sort of the Ugly Duckling of our family, and kept waiting for him to find his niche, the place he could shine, but he hasn't. He's not athletic and daring like his twin. And our cousins are hard to compete with. Poor Derrick isn't heroic like Alex. He doesn't have Nicholas's charm or Joseph's economic savvy, and he can't pull off Reese's in-your-face independence. There's nothing he's *best* at," she finished sadly. "And he's always needed to be best at something."

Stacy cocked her head to one side. "It's easy to forget how insightful you can be. You travel at such a gallop most of the time that insight has to shake a leg to keep up."

"Well, thanks." Claudia's forehead wrinkled. "I think."

"But don't you see? With all this other stuff going on, this is a bad time to get involved with someone like Ethan Mallory."

"No, I don't see." Claudia glanced around the kitchen. The cell phone did not seem to be in there. "I'm having a grand time. Nothing like mind-blowing sex to take one's mind off one's problems."

"When have you ever gone into a relationship just for sex?"

She blinked. "I didn't mean that it's *just* about sex."

"What else can it be about when you start out by agreeing that it's only temporary? Do you have a clue how you really feel about the man?"

"Good grief. Not every relationship has to lead to marriage. It would be darned confusing if they all did, wouldn't it?" She started for the living room. Maybe she'd left the phone in there. "You're making too much of this."

Stacy followed. "You don't do temporary, not with people. I'm not the only friend you've kept since grade school."

"So maybe Ethan and I will stay friends when the affair is over." That thought made her smile. She felt good with Ethan, alive yet comfortable, like being with a good friend, only with lots of sizzle. Surely they could hold on to the friendship after the sizzle part was over...somehow.

Stacy shook her head. "Some people manage that. Wanda Ellis, for example. She's remained friends with two ex-husbands and several former lovers. But are you friends with any of your former boyfriends?"

"Uh..." The doorbell chimed. "That will be Ethan," she said brightly.

"You told me he was picking you up at four!"

"I lied. I want you to meet him."

"Two's company, three's annoying." Stacy spun and started back to the kitchen. "And my frozen things are thawing. I'll stay out of sight until the two of you leave."

"No, you won't." Claudia grabbed Stacy's arm. "Come on, be brave. Maybe you'll stop worrying so much once you know Ethan. At the very least you'll have a different image in your mind when you warn me about him. Hard to think he isn't an ass,'' she said cheerfully, ''when all you can remember about him is that pretty butt of his, isn't it?''

Stacy groaned. ''Now, that just guarantees what I'll think of when I see him.''

''You were going to, anyway. Now, stay put.'' Claudia went to the door and peeped through the spy hole. ''Oh, good. He wore the yellow shirt. Canary yellow is an excellent color for Ethan,'' she informed Stacy as she undid the various locks and opened the door. ''Even if it is November.'' She forgot about colors and shirts and everything except the happy bump her heart gave.

''Hi,'' he said softly, and bent to brush her lips with his.

''Mmm.'' She realized her eyes had drifted closed and made them open. ''Come on in and meet someone.'' She stepped aside. ''This is Stacy. Whom you haven't *quite* met, though you sort of intersected with her on Monday.''

''That's one way to put it.'' Ethan's smile was charmingly rueful. ''Stacy, I hope you'll forget about our previous intersection and let me start from scratch.''

Stacy was staring up at him, owl-eyed. ''It's worse than I thought.''

Not the best beginning, but it *was* a beginning. ''You two can get acquainted while I look for my phone,'' Claudia said cheerfully. ''I need to make some calls on the way to your aunt's house, Ethan. I've had the most splendid idea.''

* * *

"You really think you can mend a feud that started before you were born by giving a surprise party tonight?" Ethan asked as he turned off on his aunt's street. "There's a lot of room for a misfire, considering that it's your own family you're surprising."

"Don't exaggerate, Ethan. I let Aunt Moira know the Contis would be coming."

"And she was perfectly happy with having five or so of your family's avowed enemies drop in on a family discussion?"

"Well…I wouldn't say she was *happy* about it. But once I'd invited them, there wasn't much she could do."

"Yes, I think I heard you pointing that out to her."

"Thank you for calling Sal Conti. I'm sure he'll be able to persuade most of his family to attend. Though I rather hope old Lucia Conti chooses not to darken a Barone door." Claudia shrugged. "If she does show up, I'll find a corner for her to cackle in."

He couldn't keep from grinning, but shook his head. "I predict fireworks tonight. Ah, looks like we're here." He pulled to a stop one door down from his aunt's house and tried to ignore the sinking feeling in his gut. Why had he let his uncle maneuver him into doing this? Claudia was never going to fit in. She'd be uncomfortable, and so would most of his family.

As usual, she hopped out as soon as the car stopped. He climbed out more slowly. From a yard away he could hear the sounds of the party—children's high-pitched voices, music from the backyard. Opera. Ethan grimaced. Aunt Sophia had an unfortunate passion for opera. The air was nippy heading toward cold, but the sky had dried out and the sun was shining.

In the clear autumn air, Claudia's hair gleamed like spun gold. But it didn't shine more brightly than her eyes when she smiled at him. "Traffic was kind to us today. We're on time."

Something kicked Ethan square in the chest. Something hard and strong and bodiless, and maybe fatal. Something that he couldn't see or touch or taste, but he knew the words for it.

He was in love with her.

What is this? he asked himself, panicked. He couldn't be in love. He knew better, damn it. This was a woman whose leaving would cut deep—and of course she would leave. What did they have in common, other than incredible sex? Even if they could somehow merge their worlds—and he didn't see how that was possible—he was accumulating evidence against her brother, for God's sake.

But if it wasn't love, what was it? He didn't just want her until his eyes crossed and his tongue got hard. He *liked her.* A lot.

He liked the way she dug into everything she did, stubborn as a bulldog. And the way she tried to fix everything for everyone. He liked her sense of humor, and the fierce loyalty she felt toward her family. He looked forward to seeing her come charging into his office every morning, full of energy, plans and instructions. And he didn't want to think of what his life would be like when she wasn't in it anymore.

He didn't want to lose her.

"Ethan? What is it? You have the funniest look on

your face. Like the old woman who swallowed a spider."

He made an effort to pull himself together. "And it wiggled and giggled and tickled inside her?"

"That's the one." She grinned. "I guess we share the same taste in fine music."

"Yeah." Well, they did have that much in common. They'd listened to the same goofy children's rhymes as kids. Suddenly he didn't want to go to the stupid party at all. He didn't need to see how impossible it would be to blend their worlds. "Listen, maybe this was a bad idea."

"What?"

"This party. You won't enjoy hanging out with a bunch of people you don't know. Especially my uncle Harold. No one enjoys him. And the kids...you'll probably get grape Kool-Aid spilled on that pretty sweater."

"It's cotton. Fully washable. And that isn't what made you look so weird. What's really wrong? Are you afraid that going to a family birthday party together makes us seem...well, too much of a couple?" She patted his arm. "Don't worry. I'm not reading anything into it."

Why the hell not? "Never mind," he growled. "Hell. Let's get it over with."

Eleven

She fit in beautifully.

Ethan watched her fend off a toddler's ice cream bar and his cousin Brad's advances with equal aplomb and no hurt feelings. She did great with his other cousins, too. When Maura's engagement ring went missing, Claudia was the one who suggested they check the trap under the sink, since Maura had been washing dishes earlier. She would have removed the trap, too, if the men of the family would have allowed such a thing. She steered newly graduated Brian to a prospective job, promising to call her friend and put in a good word for him. And when Uncle Harold and Uncle Matt squared off for their usual argument, she diverted Harold's attention long enough for Aunt Sophia to drag Matt away.

Diverting Uncle Harold's attention qualified her for

hero status with his family. When, shortly before they left, Aunt Adele had asked him if he was going to let this one slip through his fingers, he'd said, "Not if I can help it."

Claudia had told his cousin Amy that he was *sensitive.* He'd nearly spilled his beer. Amy had hooted, but when Claudia explained—rather heatedly—how understanding he'd been when she cried, Amy had actually agreed. And Ethan had tiptoed back down the hall so they wouldn't know he'd eavesdropped.

It seemed she could fit into his world just fine. Things were almost perfect…except that the reverse wasn't necessarily true.

"Your friend didn't like me much," Ethan said.

They were in his car, and he was leaning hard on the speed limit. They were going to make it to the Barone family meeting, he thought, but just barely. Not that he minded being a little late, but Claudia should have been fretting.

She wasn't. In fact, she'd been the one to delay, lingering over coffee and birthday cake. She was a lot more anxious about this gathering of the two feuding families than she wanted to admit. Or maybe she dreaded finding out about what her brother was up to.

"Stacy was a little nervous about meeting you," Claudia assured him.

"That explains it. I wondered why she took one look at me and groaned, 'It's worse than I thought.' Nerves."

She chuckled. "Stacy *is* a bit of a worrier."

Which meant, he supposed, that Stacy didn't approve of him. Or at least of his having an affair with her friend. No surprise there, he thought, signaling for the turn onto Mount Vernon Street. Just look at where he was taking her for this little get-together—Beacon Hill.

This family gathering was likely to be a lot less pleasant than the one this afternoon. And at this one, he and Claudia wouldn't be seen as a couple. That was for the best, he told himself as he crept along the street, looking for a parking space. As far as Claudia's family was concerned, he was the detective she was keeping an eye on, nothing more. He'd have to remember to keep his hands off her.

"Lots of cars," he said. Lots of house, too, he thought as they passed her aunt and uncle's town house. It was a tall, narrow, federal-style building with tall windows and two chimneys that he could see from the street.

"It looks like my parents are here already. And Nicholas." She bit her lip. "I don't know what any of the Contis' cars look like."

"Doesn't look like they're here yet. It's straight up seven o'clock now." Ethan had asked Sal to show up at quarter after to give Claudia time to explain to her family why she'd invited the Contis to attend a Barone powwow. Ethan was looking forward to hearing that explanation himself.

"Right." She relaxed slightly. "I told Aunt Moira I'd be here before the Contis arrived."

"She could probably use your help. Kind of a ticklish situation for a hostess." He wasn't really worried about a Conti-Barone confrontation, and he didn't think Claudia was, either. It was her blasted brother that had her fretting, and he didn't know what he could do to help.

As it turned out, they weren't the last to arrive. They met another couple at the top of the flagstone path leading to the door—a pretty little brunette with a shy smile and a brawny fellow in jeans and a leather jacket.

"Emily." Claudia hurried forward to give her sister a hug. "You look radiant. Being engaged agrees with you."

"Shane agrees with me," she said softly, casting her fiancé a mischievous smile. "Sometimes, anyway."

Claudia laughed. "Ethan, this is my sister, Emily, and her fiancé, Shane Cummings. Emily, Shane, this is Ethan Mallory."

"The detective?" Shane's eyebrows lifted.

"That's me. And you'd be the fireman who rescued the damsel in distress." Ethan smiled at Emily. "Glad to meet you. I'd like to talk later, if we have a chance."

She looked wary. "I don't think I can help you. I've never remembered anything from the night of the fire."

"I'm hoping you'd consider hypnosis."

She exchanged a glance with her fiancé. Shane said, "If the amnesia has a physical cause, that won't help."

"True. But then at least you'd know for sure."

Emily nodded and agreed cautiously to think about it, and the four of them proceeded to the door, with Emily and Shane ahead. Ethan murmured to Claudia, "Are you sure she's your sister?"

Claudia grinned. "We don't seem much alike, do

we? Emily is every bit as stubborn as I am, though. She just goes about it more quietly.''

The town house was even more impressive inside. Very Old World, Ethan thought as he stepped inside, with an antique table gracing the foyer that he would have given his eyeteeth for. He liked buildings and furniture with a few years on them, a little history.

He glanced at Claudia, who was passing her coat to the maid. Except for the white velvet love seat, which bore such pleasant memories for him, her apartment was furnished in a strictly modern style.

Did they have *anything* in common?

He was feeling gloomy as he entered the parlor. It held a cozy fire burning in the fireplace, several more antiques, including a Victorian sofa and two wing chairs...and what seemed like dozens of Barones. All of whom turned to stare at him.

There was a moment's awkward hush. Claudia broke it. ''*That* is the sort of silence that falls when the person one has been talking about suddenly enters the room,'' she observed. ''Was it me or Ethan you've been discussing?''

Ethan had never met the tall, lean man who stood near the fireplace, but the sharp features and sour expression were familiar. Derrick Barone lifted a glass half full of some dark liquor in a mocking toast. ''You *and* your new lover, actually. I saw him leaving your apartment at a very early hour last Wednesday, dear, and I've made some inquiries. As I've just been explaining to everyone.''

Ethan went very still.

''And did you explain why that would be any of

your business?” Claudia asked sweetly. “Because I’d like a recap of those reasons.”

“Oh, come now, Claudia. That should be obvious. Something of a conflict of interest, isn’t it? When the family asked you to keep an eye on Mallory, they didn’t mean you should favor him with other body parts, too.”

Ethan clenched his hands into fists, but he held on to his temper. He couldn’t punch Claudia’s brother out. Not here and now. But if one of her relatives didn’t do something soon—

“That’s enough, Derrick,” said a short, stocky man—Paul Barone, Claudia’s father. “There’s no need to be unpleasant.”

Nicholas muttered something to the woman beside him, who had her hand on his arm. His mother apparently overheard him. “Not in my living room, you won’t,” Moira Barone said tartly.

Claudia hadn’t said a word. Ethan forced his hands to relax and looked at her. There was a stunned, glassy look in her eyes he didn’t like. No reason for his hands off policy now, he decided, and slid an arm around her waist. “Just don’t try to smile,” he muttered close to her ear.

She made a choked sound, and damned if her lips didn’t twitch.

“Look, I’m sorry.” Derrick spread one hand wide. “I was out of line. This is why I wanted to have this discussion without Claudia—it’s bound to be painful for her. I’m worried about the repercussions from this affair for Baronessa, for all of us, but I’m worried about Claudia, too. I’d hoped we could agree to stage an intervention.”

"A *what?*" Ethan said, incredulous.

"Like when friends and family confront an alcoholic, I take it," one of the women said dryly. "You think Mallory is addictive?"

Another woman giggled.

"Let's try to be serious," Derrick snapped. "We all know Claudia's record with men isn't good. I don't want her hurt. Am I the only one who's worried that Mallory is using her to further his investigation?"

"That is just not true." Claudia took a step forward, bristling like an angry hen. "*You* might do that sort of thing. Ethan wouldn't."

Derrick looked pained. "Of course you believe that. You'll excuse me if I don't take your word for Mallory's, ah, integrity."

"I'm not sure you know the meaning of the word!" Claudia said hotly.

"Enough." That came from a tall, thin woman to Ethan's right—Sandra Barone. She spoke softly, but with sufficient authority that Claudia closed her mouth on whatever she'd been about to say. "Derrick, your sister is a big girl, and she's quite right—her affairs are none of your business."

Carlo Barone shook his head. "I am embarrassed. Is this what you've brought us together for? To make trouble for your sister?"

Derrick rounded on him, his eyes flashing. "For God's sake, Uncle Carlo! I know she's the fair-haired child, but you can't depend on her to keep an eye on Mallory now. He could be feeding her any kind of garbage in between kisses."

Ethan had had enough. "What a revolting image. But you weren't an English major, so maybe you have a little trouble with metaphors.'' He moved forward, slow and easy. ''Let's see if I understand. You'd like your family to appoint *you* to monitor my investigation?''

Derrick's lip lifted in a sneer. ''Me, or someone else you aren't f—''

Ethan's hand shot out and closed on Derrick's shoulder. And squeezed. ''I'll keep this simple. Shut up.''

The blood drained from Derrick's face. His mouth opened and closed. He tried to jerk loose, and couldn't. Ethan kept squeezing, feeling bone grate beneath his hand—then let go with a little shove. Derrick staggered backward.

Ethan spoke very softly. ''Listen up. No one monitors my investigation. I report to my employer. I use assistants I trust. I trust Claudia. I don't like or trust you. If I see you within spitting distance of me, I'm liable to get upset.''

Derrick rubbed his shoulder, his face mottled with fury. ''Stupid jock! Too dumb for anything but brute force, aren't you?'' He turned in a half circle, addressing the others. ''Are you going to let him get away with that? Is he allowed to brutalize me in front of all my dear relatives?''

''Brutality is what you can expect from Ethan,'' said a cool, feminine voice from the doorway. ''My compliments. Apparently he's cowed all the Barones except you.''

Ethan shook his head and sighed. This was just what his evening needed to be complete. ''Hello, Bianca.''

* * *

Claudia supposed she must have spent a worse evening at some point in her life, but she couldn't call any examples to mind.

No one had been happy with Derrick—well, no one but Bianca. The two of them had huddled in a corner with their heads together, no doubt having a great time disliking everyone else.

But however much the family hadn't appreciated Derrick's methods, his poison had still worked. If she'd had to listen to one more word of gentle advice before they left, she would have screamed.

Screaming still had a lot of appeal. But not until she got home. She didn't want to startle Ethan into wrecking his car. "I like your family better than mine," she muttered.

"You're forgetting Uncle Harold."

She snorted. "Quit trying to make me laugh. I'm wallowing in self-pity. I don't do this very often, so when I do succumb, I like to give it my full attention."

"Acquiring a new skill does take a lot of concentration."

"Mmm." Derrick had been so different tonight. Almost out of control. He'd been unpleasant enough in front of everyone, but before he left he'd managed to speak to her privately, and then he'd been really ugly. He'd been so angry! "Selling out the family" had been the least vile of his accusations. His words had hurt her, but it had been the look in his eyes that frightened her.

Of course, Derrick had always been difficult. Self-absorbed. But she couldn't remember him being cruel before.

Claudia sighed. Sometimes she thought there was nothing Derrick craved more than the approval of his family, yet he went out of his way to antagonize everyone. What made him be that way?

No, she thought with a painful stab of honesty. The real question, the one eating at her, was what *she* had done to make him the way he was. Or not done. How could she have failed to notice how troubled he was? Maybe if she'd been more supportive, listened more patiently to his schemes, paid more attention when he needed it…but it had been easier not to reach out, and call that neglect tolerance.

She couldn't remember the last time she'd phoned him just to chat. Or asked him to meet her for lunch. Guilt rose, sick and choking. She'd been so busy fixing everyone else's problems, she'd ignored her own brother.

"Do your folks have lots of antiques the way your aunt and uncle do?"

Ethan's question pulled her out of her thoughts. "What? Oh, yes, quite a few. Though Mother is more into 'Old Boston' than Old World."

"You aren't into old things. Your apartment is modern."

"You know how it is. When I moved out I wanted my place to be different from my parents', so I went for a contemporary look."

"I guess you're pretty tired of antiques, having grown up around them."

"No, not really. I've been thinking it would be nice to blend in a few older pieces. They have so much character." She sighed. "I really sabotaged myself, didn't I? I picked the wrong night to bring the Contis and Barones together."

"Hey, it didn't go that badly."

"Sal Conti called Uncle Carlo a sanctimonious jackass. He had some excuse, since Uncle Carlo had just called him a 'nosybody' with nothing better to do than hire detectives to stick their noses into other people's business."

"I thought their insults were pretty creative."

"I'm so glad I could inspire creativity, but that wasn't *quite* my goal."

"Hey." He reached across the seat and caught her hand. "They were talking. That's more than they've done in a lot of years. They did settle down and just glare at each other after a while. And Steven Conti seemed willing to bury the feud."

"He did, didn't he?" She brightened slightly. "He was very friendly."

Ethan gave her a level glance. "How friendly?"

"Nice friendly, not come-on friendly. Ethan, this isn't the way to my apartment."

"Son of a gun. You're right."

"In fact, this is the way to your place."

"Mine is closer than yours."

"Ethan." She was exasperated. "You're supposed to ask, not assume. I've had a stressful evening. I'm afraid I'm not in the mood for company right now."

"Do you really want to be alone tonight? I'll take you to your place and drive away—if you're sure that's what you want. But I have another plan I'd like you to consider."

Something in his voice made her heart give a little jump.

"See, I know you said you want to be allowed to brood without distractions. I'm sorry to say I can't allow that. Oh, you can brood if you want. And you don't have to talk. In fact, I think it's best that you do nothing at all. I'll take care of everything."

"What…ah, if you're talking about what I think you're talking about, that's a *mutual* activity. Pleasure given and received."

"You don't have to worry about pleasing me, Claudia. You do that just by breathing. And tonight you don't have to do a thing. Actually," he said, slowing and signaling his turn, "you aren't allowed to do anything."

"Not allowed?" Her voice squeaked.

"That's right. Here's what I had in mind. As soon as my apartment door closes behind us, I'm stripping you. You just stand there and let me do whatever I want to. I'll probably want to take my time about it, so I can enjoy the parts I uncover."

"You—" She had to stop and swallow. "You're assuming a lot."

He went on as if she hadn't spoken. "Then, when you're all nice and naked—I've been wanting to get you naked for hours—I'm carrying you to my bed and laying you down. I love the way you look in my bed, so I may want to just appreciate the sight of you there for a moment. Then I'll start kissing you. Can you guess where I want to kiss you?"

Maybe the place that was getting all quivery and warm. Very warm.

"I'm not sure myself where I'll start. There isn't a place on you I don't enjoy tasting. Maybe the backs of your knees. You're very sensitive there, aren't you? But then there's your neck. I like biting you there. And your nipples. Lord, I love it when they're all hard and rosy—"

"Ethan—"

"Hush now. You aren't supposed to talk. This is one time you won't be in charge, Claudia. Now, where was I? Oh, yes. Your nipples. Yes, I'll want to suck them, but I may save that for a bit. Your breasts are so pretty. I might just nibble my way in toward the peaks. The skin is so creamy on the undersides. I can only think of one other place that's as soft as the skin on the undersides of your breasts. It's a lot creamier, though. Hot and wet and creamy. In fact—"

"Ethan!"

"In fact, I may just start there. Skip the appetizers. Go straight to the best part."

"Ethan," she ordered, "drive faster."

They didn't make it to his bed. Ethan tried. He managed to strip her slowly, and oh, yes, she was beautiful standing by his front door, all flushed and naked. And quivering. She was deeply aroused, and he'd hardly touched her.

So was he. That was why his plan to distract her backfired.

It had torn him up to see the lost, unhappy look in her eyes after Derrick staged his little show, and he hadn't known what to say to make things better. Because things weren't going to get better with her brother.

So he'd laid his plan to sidetrack her, and he'd succeeded. Wildly. But it backfired, because he was just as distracted. Or crazy. He found he couldn't resist improvising. Once he had her naked, he just had to taste her…right where he knew she was hoping he would. He dropped to his knees in front of her and told her to open her legs wider.

It was a wonder how obedient she could be sometimes.

The taste and smell of her, the sounds she made, the way she threaded her fingers in his hair—she made him crazy. He'd meant to stop, but he couldn't. Then she came apart. Just flat buckled, and would have sunk to the floor if he hadn't scooped her up in his arms.

Claudia was barely aware of Ethan sliding his arms under her when her legs gave way. Her mind was gone, had floated out somewhere on a hazy pleasure breeze, the little zephyr that lingered after the big storm had hit and run. Her body was wrecked. Worthless. She'd never felt so helpless in her life, yet she was smiling when he laid her on his couch.

"Mmm," she said, and managed to lift a hand to stroke his cheek, where a hint of beard stubble made her fingertips tingle.

He caught her hand and pressed a kiss into her palm. "You just lie here, honey, and let me look at you."

That wasn't right. She was supposed to make him feel good, too. She tried to tug his head down for a kiss, rustling up the energy to get her other hand into the act.

He did kiss her, and she tasted herself on his lips. A little thrill of wicked pleasure opened her eyes wider. She slid her hands down to his shoulders. He was still fully dressed.

"Uh-uh." His voice was raspy and tender. He took her hands and stretched them over her head. "Breathe, Claudia. That's all you have to do tonight. It's my turn to fix things."

Fix things? She wasn't sure what he meant, but he definitely was in a mood to arrange things. First her arms went over her head. He stepped back, looking at her. He was breathing quick and light. Then he arranged her legs to suit him—one bent at the knee, the other with the foot trailing onto the floor. He smiled.

She smiled back, feeling strangely suspended by a warm swell of feeling, a rising tide as gentle as it was irresistible.

He tore off two buttons getting rid of his clothes.

Then he was sinking into her, thick and pulsing. How odd it was, she thought hazily, to lie back and let the pleasure happen, neither courting nor refusing it, responsible for nothing but her breath. How odd to be the one given to, not the one giving. So different…and liberating.

Ethan wouldn't be hurried. Not that she felt the least hasty herself. As he thrust into her in an easy rhythm, her thoughts splintered and floated away. Her hips rose languorously to meet his. She touched his hair, his face, and fell into wonderment almost as strong as the huge, rolling wave of pleasure that finally lifted her and broke, peaceful and perfect, just as he groaned and ground into her one last time.

The upholstery on his couch was rougher than her velvet love seat's. But the couch was much bigger, big enough for him to collapse beside her and gather her close in his arms. She lay quietly, smiling and smiling. Wishing she had the words to tell him what a perfect gift he'd given her.

Amazing that she'd been able to surrender control to him that way. She'd never been able—never even been tempted—to do that before. If she didn't know better, she'd think…

Alarm prickled over her skin. She stirred. No, that was absurd. She'd only known him ten days. Ten days was not enough time for—for anything *momentous* to happen. Relationships took time and care and—

"Are you back?" His voice was deep and quiet, his mouth so close to her ear that she felt the rumble of it as much as she heard it.

"Mmm." She stretched one leg, then the other. "Mostly. That was…" She rubbed her foot along his calf. "Incredible."

"Yes, you are." He kissed her ear and snuggled her up even closer.

A little tingle sped through her, but it wasn't desire. More like fear. This felt too right. Too perfect. As if she could spend the next two or three years just like this, wrapped in Ethan's arms.

Oh, God. She'd done it to herself again.

"Something wrong?"

She made herself relax, or tried to. "Of course not. I do need to get home soon, though."

"No, you don't. In a few minutes I'll have the energy to carry you to my bed. That's where you belong." He propped himself up on one elbow to smile down at her. "Honey, if you're worrying about all that temporary stuff I talked about, forget it. I've changed my mind."

"You have."

He nodded, still smiling tenderly. "I think we should get married."

The sizzle that jolted her upright was unmistakable—pure, undiluted panic. Straight up, no chaser. "I'm going home now."

Twelve

Ethan watched as the warm, loving woman in his arms bolted out of them in a total tizzy.

"I have an appointment in the morning," Claudia said, casting about for her clothes. "I can't stay over tonight, I'm afraid. Oh, there they are." She grabbed her panties from the floor.

"What the hell do you think you're doing?" he growled, sitting up. "I just proposed to you, dammit!"

"No, you didn't!" She had her panties on and was hopping on one foot, trying to get the other into the leg of her pants. "You *told* me what we should do!"

"So I wasn't romantic. So sue me." He hurt so much, his chest ached with it. He muttered something his aunt would have washed his mouth out with soap for and pushed to his feet. "Stop scrambling into your clothes and talk. Dammit, we have to talk about this."

''I don't *have* to do anything. Stop throwing orders at me.'' She had her lower half covered and reached for her bra. ''Anyway, you don't want to marry me.''

''The hell I don't!'' He grabbed for her—and snagged her bra instead when she twisted away. ''Blast it all, Claudia, hold still!''

''I am not the kind of woman who marries a man she's only known for ten days. It's ridiculous. It's...you'll be glad, later, that I didn't let you actually propose. You'll be glad. You'll see.'' Her eyes were frantic. Her hair was a tangled mess down her back. ''Give me my bra.''

He decided to try soothing her. ''You're getting all worked up, honey. Calm down.''

''Don't tell me to be calm! I'll be hysterical if I want to!''

Ethan made a big mistake then. He knew it was a mistake, but he couldn't help it. She looked so cute and so silly, standing there half dressed and spitting mad, her hands fisted at her sides and her pretty breasts heaving.

He laughed.

She threw the phone book at him.

He fended it off easily enough, but her choice of weapons did nothing to quell his amusement. ''Come on, honey. You can't go anywhere. You don't have a car.'' Or her bra, which he still held.

She pulled her sweater on over her bare chest. ''I'll get a cab.''

''Don't be ridiculous. If you insist on leaving, I'll take you back to your place.'' He reached for his jeans. ''Damned crazy woman—hey, come back here!''

She'd grabbed her purse and was fumbling with the locks on the door. "Don't you tell me what to do!"

He hopped on one leg, trying to get his other foot inserted into the inside-out leg of his jeans. "We're going to talk about this reasonably if I have to tie you down!"

She flung the door open. Cold air from his tiny vestibule swept in. "I don't know why you'd think for a second you wanted to marry me. You must know I'll never put up with your caveman tactics."

"Because I love you!" he roared.

"I love you, too, you overgrown ape!" she screamed. And slammed the door shut behind her.

She loved him? Ethan stood there with his jeans half on, grinning like a fool. How about that. Claudia loved him.

She loved him, and he was standing here while she walked out on him?

He started forward, stumbled over his jeans, cursed and peeled them off and ran after her.

He got there just in time. She had the front door open. When he slammed open his door she froze there in the doorway, her eyes round. "Ethan," she whispered. "You're naked."

"No kidding." The vestibule was damned cold, a chilly wind shriveling the part of him that wasn't usually exposed to such things. He could only hope his upstairs tenants didn't feel a sudden need to come downstairs. "We're going to talk about this," he insisted stubbornly.

"Yes. All right." She kept darting little glances up the stairs, then back to him. "But later. In about six months, maybe, when we've had time to know each other better.''

''Now. We're going to talk about it now.''

''No,'' she said, her chin tilting up. She blinked, but not quickly enough for him to miss the telltale gleam of tears in her eyes. ''We aren't.'' And she dashed out onto the sidewalk.

He almost went after her. It was the sight of those damp eyes, more than any sensible reluctance to race outside naked, that stopped him. But it was the sound of a door closing upstairs that sent him back inside his apartment. Where he paced.

Claudia loved him, but for some reason that made her cry. When he asked her to marry him, she had a panic attack. All right, he conceded, maybe he hadn't exactly asked. Maybe it had been—he winced—a sorry excuse for a proposal. But that didn't explain her reaction.

He sighed. He'd rushed her, that much was obvious. She wanted to go more slowly, and on the surface of it, he couldn't blame her. But dammit, he didn't have much time. He sure couldn't wait any six months. He'd told his uncle that Claudia wasn't like Bianca, and dammit, she wasn't. She wouldn't walk out on him once she'd given him her promise.

But he was closing in on her brother. This afternoon, his uncle had taken him aside for a minute.

He'd found Norblusky.

Claudia was humming when the cab let her out in front of Ethan's office at eleven o'clock the next morning. That made her think of him, and that made her pause and smile.

He'd run out after her stark, staring naked. A man who would do that, she thought as she climbed the stairs, was slightly crazy. But it was a nice sort of nuts, not the temporary kind that sometimes made men say things they didn't really mean because they were basking in a sexual afterglow. No, Ethan hadn't been glowing at all by then. He'd been furious.

She grinned happily. And he'd *still* wanted to talk about marriage.

Viewed from the clarity of morning, her reaction last night was a bit embarrassing.

Claudia fitted the key she'd talked Rick into loaning her in the lock and swung open the office door. Ethan wouldn't be in today. He'd told her at his aunt's house yesterday that he had to take care of one of his other cases.

Poor man. He was getting discouraged, she thought as she set down her purse and shrugged out of her coat. After all his work, Norblusky was still missing, and they hadn't turned up any new leads in the past couple of days.

Well, the police hadn't found the man, either, or made any progress with the arson. Obviously Norblusky was a good deal smarter than Ethan seemed to think. Claudia hoped that, by going over everything they'd collected so far, she could come up with an idea to pursue.

It was only as she sat in Ethan's big wooden chair that she realized something odd. The overhead lights were on. And the computer. She put her palm on the CPU beneath the desk. The monitor was dark, but the CPU was turned on.

Had Ethan changed his mind and come in? If so,

where was he? She frowned and tapped her fingers on the desk. Surely they were past the point where he'd try to shut her out of the investigation.

Beside her, the fax machine chattered. She swiveled, still frowning. She really shouldn't read whatever was coming in. That would be like reading someone else's personal mail. Still, Ethan did seem to have pulled some sort of trick this morning, claiming he wasn't coming into the office. She'd take a quick look, she decided. Just a glance to see if it had something to do with the case.

The first page finished printing. She leaned forward and plucked it from the document holder. It was a copy of a bank statement for someone named Guy Amberson. Did this have something to do with the investigation, or not?

Wait a minute. Whoever this Guy Amberson was, he'd made quite a large deposit the day after the gelato tampering. Seventy-five thousand dollars. In *cash.*

Oh, this was definitely connected. And Ethan hadn't told her a thing about it. Simmering, she snatched up the next sheet as soon as the fax machine spat it out. Another bank statement, this one for a different month—the month of the arson at the plant—and the fax was still printing.

In all, she collected five bank statements. And an invoice.

The invoice was from someone named Ernie. He was billing Ethan for acquiring copies of "bank statements showing activity in the past twelve months for the account of Guy Amberson, aka Derrick Barone."

Claudia's fingers went cold. The paper fluttered to the floor.

The office door opened. ''What the— Claudia? How did you get in?''

She met Ethan's eyes. The cold was spreading. ''A key. I used Rick's key.''

His eyes flicked to the paper she'd dropped, then to the others on the desk. He stood very still and didn't say a word.

''You know what this is, don't you?'' She shoved back the chair and stood. ''Bank statements supposedly belonging to my brother. Fraudulent, of course. Derrick's difficult, but he isn't—he wouldn't do this. Not this.''

''My information broker is completely reliable. Whatever he sends is the real thing.'' Ethan came up to the desk. He picked up one of the bank statements and scanned it quickly. He sighed and let it drop. ''I'm sorry, Claudia.''

''This Guy Amberson isn't Derrick!'' she said furiously. ''Someone is trying to make you think it was my brother. Just how did you come across this—this fake bank statement, anyway?''

His voice was as wooden as his face. ''From the information broker I use. As I said, he's reliable. The bank statements are real.''

''Okay, even if they're real statements, that doesn't mean this Guy person is my brother.''

''I'm afraid...'' He paused for a long moment. ''Claudia, yesterday my uncle found Ed Norblusky.''

Her breath caught. ''Y-you didn't tell me. Why didn't you tell me?''

''Norblusky's sister has been receiving payments from him. Rent for a little cottage in the woods. My uncle got a copy of one of the checks and used that to trace him.'' He paused. ''Norblusky talked. He told Uncle Thomas who paid him to hide. And who told him what route to take on the day someone poured pepper juice on the gelato for the tasting.''

''No.'' She shook her head. ''He's lying, Ethan. I don't know why. Maybe someone paid him to say those things.''

''He received a check from Guy Amberson for his cooperation. My uncle took a picture of Derrick to the bank that check was drawn on. One of the tellers identified him as Amberson. She remembered him because he flirted with her.''

Her breathing wasn't working right. She came out from behind his desk, needing to do something. Anything. To prove to him how wrong he was. ''We have to tell Derrick. Someone is framing him. He has to know.''

''No.''

''He has to know. You can't expect me not to tell him.''

He looked suddenly, terribly weary. ''I knew you would want to. That's why I didn't tell you my uncle found Norblusky.''

''You didn't tell me your uncle was even looking for him. I thought Thomas was retired.''

''He is. He just takes on a job for me now and then.''

She digested that. It went down slow and painful, like crumbs of glass. ''How much else haven't you been telling me? The other cases you've said you were working on sometimes…"

He didn't answer. And that was answer enough. "Oh, God." She turned away, pacing to the window and staring out blindly. "You've been after Derrick all along, haven't you?" And he wouldn't listen to her, didn't believe that someone had set all this up. But that was the only possible explanation.

She thought of her parents. Her sister and their other brother. Her aunt and uncle and Nicholas. And all the others… "This is going to be horrible," she whispered, hugging her middle. "Ethan, please. I'm begging you. Someone must have framed Derrick, and I d-don't know how to prove it. I need you."

"There's no frame." His voice was raw. "I've checked and double-checked everything."

In other words—no. He wouldn't help her. She blinked fiercely, determined not to cry. "When you were supposedly working on other cases, you mean."

A pause, followed by a sigh. "Yes. The evidence is solid, Claudia. Derrick used his Guy Amberson alias to buy the habanero pepper juice. He paid Norblusky. He has no alibi for the night of the arson—"

"And you have no evidence!" She spun around. "Do you? Not about the arson."

"Not yet. But I have to give what I've got to the police, Claudia. Once they're concentrating on Derrick—under whatever name—it will be just a matter of time before they can connect him."

"You're wrong." He had to be wrong. Sickly, she realized she could conceive of Derrick having taken a bribe to ruin Baronessa's new flavor. No one had ever appreciated him, in his opinion. He'd been shuttled aside, denied the big corner office he wanted… But not the fire. "Good grief, Emily was injured in the fire! You can't believe he would hurt her."

"He probably didn't know she was at the plant."

But Claudia wasn't listening. Thinking of her sister had diverted her. "Ethan, you thought Emily might be able to remember under hypnosis."

"She might. She wasn't too crazy about the idea."

Claudia crossed to him, seizing his arm. "Don't tell the police yet. Please. Let me talk to Emily first. If she can only remember…maybe she saw something that will prove it wasn't Derrick."

He was silent for a long moment. "And if she refuses?"

"She won't. Not when she knows this is for Derrick."

The therapist's waiting room was small, maybe twelve feet on a side. Ethan watched as Claudia paced its length for the umpteenth time. She worried him.

She'd gone quiet right after talking to Emily. After Emily and Shane went into the inner office with the therapist, she'd tried sitting and looking through a magazine, but that hadn't lasted long. She'd been pacing for—Ethan glanced at his watch. Twenty-seven minutes.

Her face was pale, but two flags of color came and went every so often on her cheeks, linked to whatever internal struggle she was working out as she went up and down, up and down the small room. She seemed wholly unaware of him.

Ethan ached to hold her, comfort her, but when

he'd tried taking her hand she'd stared at him so blankly. As if she couldn't remember who he was.

He shifted. Dana's chairs were probably comfortable enough for most people, but they didn't fit a man his size very well.

Claudia had been right about one thing. Emily had agreed immediately when she understood what was at stake. Ethan had pulled some strings pretty hard to get an appointment right away—those strings being attached to his cousin Sharla, whose husband's sister was Dana. Otherwise known as Dr. Dana Merriweather.

Emily had asked that Shane be present during the session. They were in there now. Ethan stretched out his legs. They'd been in there a long time.

Claudia muttered something.

"What, honey?"

She gave him that blank stare. "Nothing. I'm just...thinking."

Probably figuring out how to break Derrick out of jail, once he got there. Ethan grimaced.

The door opened. Ethan was on his feet before he decided to stand up. Claudia stopped moving.

Emily's pallor told its own tale. So did the tear tracks on her cheeks. Shane had an arm around her protectively, but she pulled free when she saw Claudia and went to her, holding her hands out. "It worked," she said, her voice small. "I remembered."

Claudia took her sister's hands. She didn't speak. Ethan moved up behind her and rested his hands on her shoulders.

She shrugged them off.

His lips tightened. He wasn't going to give up, but this wasn't the time to push her.

"Emily?" Claudia whispered. "What did you remember?"

"I know why I was at the plant that night. I was looking for something, some kind of evidence. I'd overheard Derrick talking on his private line with someone from Snowcream, Inc. and i-it didn't sound right. But I couldn't quite believe…I didn't want to say anything without some kind of proof." Her voice trailed off. She swallowed. "It was Derrick. I saw him, though I don't think he saw me. He set the fire."

Claudia's shoulders jerked. "How could I have let it get this bad?" she whispered. "How could I not have known?"

Ethan tried to be soothing. "No one knew, honey."

"But I should have!" She flung herself away, pacing again. "I've been so busy fixing everything for everyone. But my brother, my own brother, was so desperately messed up—and I didn't know." Tears spilled from her eyes. She dashed them away angrily.

"It's not your fault!" Emily protested.

"Isn't it? I've been thinking, remembering, trying to understand how I failed—how I could have failed—"

"That's enough," Ethan snapped.

She stopped and stared at him. So did the others.

He walked up to her. "You aren't in charge of your brother. You aren't responsible for what he decided to do."

"But I should have seen! If I'd been paying attention, I would have known something was wrong. I could have helped—"

He gripped her arms. ''If it's your fault, then it's even more Emily's fault. She worked with him every day, right? Why didn't she realize he needed help? Or your parents? They must bear even more of the blame. What did they do wrong, that their son turned out this way?''

''That's a horrible thing to say!''

''Yeah.'' His voice softened. ''It is, isn't it? So why are you saying it to yourself?'' He wanted so badly to hold her close, but she was rigid beneath his hands. He had to try to put everything into his voice. ''Some things can only be fixed by the one on the inside, honey. Derrick has to fix himself. You can't do it for him.''

In the brief silence that fell, Claudia's eyes filled. And her purse rang.

''Damn.'' Her voice shook as she wiped her eyes again, without stemming the flow. ''My phone. I don't know why I brought it.''

Ethan went to the chair where she'd left the over-size leather purse she toted everywhere. Her phone was tucked into a pocket on the outside. He took it out and started to shut off the power, but happened to notice the little caller ID window. He hesitated.

Claudia sniffed. ''Who is it?''

''Your folks.''

''They never call on my cell phone. I forget to charge it or leave it at home so often...'' Her voice trailed off. ''I'd better see what they want.''

He handed it to her. Their fingers didn't touch, which took some doing with the tiny phone.

''Hello? Yes,'' she said after a moment, ''Emily is

with me. Why?'' A few seconds later every bit of color drained from her face. ''We'll be right there.''

''What is it?'' Emily asked, alarmed.

''Derrick and Bianca Conti have been kidnapped.''

Thirteen

Claudia had heard that sometimes, in the midst of battle, a soldier can be shot and not realize it right away. The body reports the blow, but the pain is oddly absent. That was what she felt like. Detached. Aware of the blow, but not yet hurting.

On their bat-out-of-hell ride to her parents' house she was mostly aware of three things: a vague queasiness in the pit of her stomach; the battle to stop thinking, which she was rapidly losing—and Ethan.

"We're almost there, honey," he said.

"Good." She glanced down at her hands, which were clasped tightly together in her lap. "Are Shane and Emily still behind us?"

"Sure are. The man's been so intimate with my bumper, our cars are practically engaged."

She tried to smile, but suspected it was a poor attempt. As were her efforts not to think. She couldn't stop, couldn't keep from following the terrible train of logic.

"Ethan?" she said as he screeched to a stop in front of her parents' house.

"Yeah?"

"Derrick probably wasn't kidnapped, was he?"

He paused, then said very gently, "No, honey. I don't think he was."

She swallowed. "And Bianca?"

"I don't know. That may be for real. We'll have to treat it as if it is."

Shane's car jerked to a halt just as Ethan climbed out of his. He hurried around to Claudia's side, and she let him put his arm around her. He was desperately glad of that. There was so damned little he could do for her. She seemed calm, but he knew that for what it was—the numbing blanket that shock spreads over its victims.

She'd staggered him. After all her denial, her defense of her brother, she'd already figured out what this kidnapping must really be: a last, frantic effort by Derrick Barone to excel at something. If he couldn't be the best at anything else, he'd be the best criminal the family had ever produced. Ethan was all but certain Derrick had faked his own kidnapping.

Claudia's mother must have been watching for them. She opened the door before the four of them reached the porch. Ethan heard the raised voices before then, too.

The three women fell into a female huddle, hugging one another. "Sal and Jean Conti are here," Sandra Barone told them. Her eyes were red. "And your aunt and uncle, and Nicholas. The others are on their way."

"I hear them." Claudia gave her mother a last hug, then detached herself gently. "I'll take care of it."

She headed for the room where all the shouting was coming from. Ethan followed her.

"...not telling me how to handle this, dammit! They've got my daughter!" Sal Conti yelled.

"And my son!" Paul Barone said furiously. "You know damned well you can't raise ten million dollars."

"This is one time your proud neck will have to bow to the inevitable," Carlo Barone said. "I can get the money. You can't. Deal with it."

"If you Barones put up the money, you'll want to call the shots! I know what you're like, and I won't have it!"

"Mr. Conti," Claudia said firmly, walking up to him. "You're shouting."

He glared at her. "Damned right I'm shouting!"

"Well, it's not helping." She took his hand in both of hers and spoke gently. "What I heard when I walked in was my uncle offering to pay ten million dollars to help you get your daughter back. That doesn't seem like something to be angry about."

Sal was taken aback, but rallied. "He'll try to take over. Dammit, you know what he's like—thinks he was born to rule. Well, I'm not having it. Those bastards have my daughter." He blinked, his voice breaking. "My Bianca."

For a second Claudia's eyes met Ethan's, and he knew the same question haunted them both. He didn't much like his ex-wife, but there were still strings, the tattered remnants of the feelings that had once propelled him willy-nilly into marriage. His mouth was dry with fear and a few lingering, acrid regrets.

Was Bianca a willing accomplice—or Derrick Barone's victim?

Claudia looked away and squeezed Sal Conti's hand. ''Naturally you want very badly to have some control over the situation. But shouting isn't the way to accomplish that.'' She looked at Carlo. ''Uncle Carlo, you agree that Mr. Conti must have an equal voice in whatever is decided, don't you?''

''It's the right thing, Carlo,'' Moira Barone said in a low voice.

He looked sour, but agreed. Then he noticed Ethan and came toward him. ''Mr. Mallory. Good. I was hoping…we may need someone to handle the, uh, the drop for us. I can pay whatever your fee is.''

''I won't take your money, so you can forget about that. Have you called the FBI?''

''No police,'' Paul Barone said sharply. ''Both ransom notes said the same thing—don't call the police. They threatened to kill—'' He stopped and swallowed. ''No police.''

''Let's talk about it,'' Ethan said in his most soothing voice. ''Put our heads together, see what we know so far. Maybe we should all sit down. Claudia, if you could see about some coffee…''

''I'll take care of it,'' she said.

The next few hours were rough. Ethan finally persuaded both families that they had to call in the FBI—in part because Claudia quietly, firmly backed him up.

They also agreed to stall for time, claim they needed a few days to get the ransom money together.

Ethan did not tell them what he knew about Derrick Barone.

Before the FBI agents arrived he made an excuse to head into the kitchen, where he used his cell phone to call his uncle. Claudia came in while he was talking. He eyed her warily as he told his uncle to be careful, and disconnected.

"You asked him to check out Norblusky's hiding place," she said quietly.

"Yeah. It's a long shot. I don't really think Norblusky would go along with anything like this, especially when he's already spilled the beans to my uncle. But it would be foolish to ignore the possibility."

"Thank you for not telling the others about Derrick. About what he's done, and—and what we think he's done."

"They'll have to know eventually, but I thought..." He shrugged, awkward and miserable about the strain in her eyes. "Seemed best to wait until I've talked to the FBI. I do have to tell them, Claudia."

"I know." Her smile was pale, nothing like her usual megawatt beam. But it seemed genuine. "In the meantime, we can try to keep this to one blow at a time for the others. Ethan..."

Something in her voice pulled him closer. "Yeah?"

She shook her head. "Nothing. I just...I'm glad you're here."

Funny. His heart actually skipped a beat. He'd never felt it do that before. "Even though—"

"Claudia?" Shane came around the corner. "Good, Ethan is with you. The FBI agents are here. They'll need to talk to you both."

Philip Ringle was the agent in charge. He seemed sharp, capable. He spoke with all of them together first, then Ethan asked to have a word with him privately.

It took nearly an hour to give the federal agent everything he had on Derrick Barone. When he finished, Ringle asked questions, then told Ethan he could leave.

Claudia was nowhere in sight. He looked in the big living room, in the kitchen, the library. No one knew where she was. Emily thought she might have gone upstairs to lie down or get a few moments alone.

It finally dawned on him that she didn't want to see him.

He could understand that, he told himself as he collected his coat. He'd give her time. Maybe she'd been grateful earlier for his presence—she knew, if the rest of her family didn't, what he'd just spent the past forty-nine minutes doing. Pointing the FBI straight at her brother.

The temperature had dropped, and the wind was icy. He turned his collar up as he trudged toward his car. Her rejection hurt. No matter how he explained it to himself, it hurt like blazes. He wondered how long it would take her to look at him and see anything except the man who'd put her brother behind bars.

Looks like snow, he thought, pausing to stare up at a sky even colder and grayer than his old Buick. *Hell!*

Why am I leaving? So she was avoiding him. She still needed him, dammit.

She had to, or his world would never be warm again. He turned away from his car.

She was running down the steps, her hair flying out behind her like a golden banner whipped by the wind. And no coat on. "Ethan! Wait!"

Hastily he stripped his coat off. The second she reached him he flung it over her shoulders. "Crazy woman! It's freezing out here."

"Well." Her smile peeped out. "At least I didn't chase after you naked."

There was an odd sensation in his chest, kind of tight and warm, as if she'd hugged him on the inside. "Probably just as well," he said gruffly. "Your parents wouldn't understand. Not that I do," he added, searching her face. And hoping. Hoping hard.

"Why aren't you holding me?" she asked softly.

He grabbed her then and held on, and he didn't notice the cold wind or the first few flakes of snow that fell. "I thought you didn't want to see me. I looked for you. No one knew where you were. Emily thought you might have gone upstairs to be alone."

"Good grief. I was in the bathroom. When I came back downstairs Emily told me you were looking for me, and then I couldn't find *you.*" She touched his jaw. Her eyes were tired, but clear. "Did you really think I blamed you for what Derrick has done? I've been foolish about a lot of things, including the kind of man who's right for me. But I do know right from wrong. What you did was right."

He swallowed. "I was afraid…I thought your feelings might be pretty mixed. I know how much your family means to you."

"They don't mean more than you do. I *love* you, Ethan."

A second later, she patted him on the shoulder. "You're going to break something if you squeeze me any tighter."

"I'm sorry. I just...I feel so good." And he wasn't sure he ought to, with all the misery cooped up in the big house behind him. But he couldn't help it. Claudia loved him. "I'll give you time," he promised. "Like you said you wanted. Time to think things out. I know we don't have much in common, and your family won't exactly be thrilled, but I'm giving you fair warning. I'm not letting you go."

"My family will be delighted. Especially if you keep me too busy to meddle in their lives. As for not having anything in common—good grief. Haven't you been paying attention? We're so much alike it's scary. You're hardheaded, always sure you're right. Just like me. You put family first, like I do. And you're always fixing things." She kissed him, lightly but lingering. "That's what you do for a living, for heaven's sake. Fix things. You're as much of a meddler as I am, only you get paid for it."

He'd never thought of it that way. It disconcerted him, so he kissed her again. Not lightly.

After a moment she said, "We'll live in your place, I think. I'd like to get married in the spring."

"That's too long to wait," he informed her, treasuring the warm weight of her body against his. "Next month."

"June."

''Christmas.''

''Valentine's Day. And you're going to wear a tux.''

Ethan laughed. He probably would.

* * * * *

DYNASTIES: THE BARONES *continues….*
Read the conclusion to the Barones saga—
1549 PASSIONATELY EVER AFTER
by Metsy Hingle
December 2003
Only from Silhouette Books!

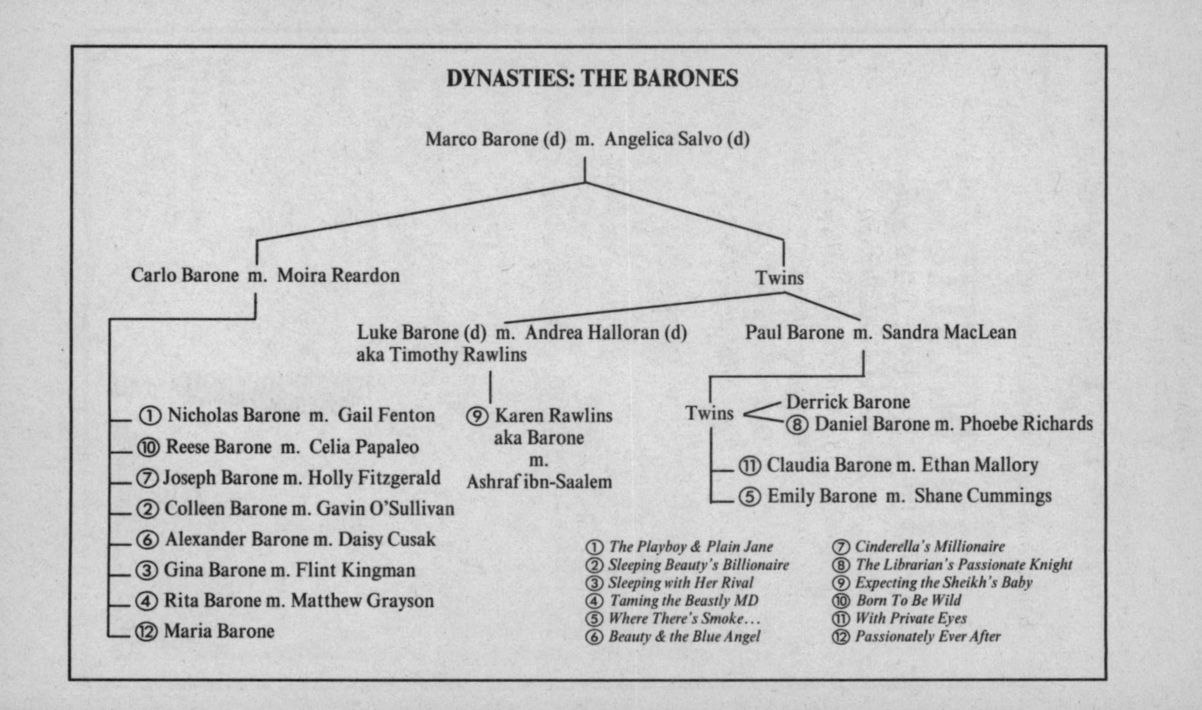
DYNASTIES: THE BARONES
Marco Barone (d) m. Angelica Salvo (d)
Carlo Barone m. Moira Reardon
Twins
Luke Barone (d) m. Andrea Halloran (d)
aka Timothy Rawlins
Paul Barone m. Sandra MacLean
① Nicholas Barone m. Gail Fenton
⑩ Reese Barone m. Celia Papaleo
⑦ Joseph Barone m. Holly Fitzgerald
② Colleen Barone m. Gavin O'Sullivan
⑥ Alexander Barone m. Daisy Cusak
③ Gina Barone m. Flint Kingman
④ Rita Barone m. Matthew Grayson
⑫ Maria Barone
⑨ Karen Rawlins
aka Barone
m.
Ashraf ibn-Saalem
Twins
Derrick Barone
⑧ Daniel Barone m. Phoebe Richards
⑪ Claudia Barone m. Ethan Mallory
⑤ Emily Barone m. Shane Cummings
① The Playboy & Plain Jane
② Sleeping Beauty's Billionaire
③ Sleeping with Her Rival
④ Taming the Beastly MD
⑤ Where There's Smoke…
⑥ Beauty & the Blue Angel
⑦ Cinderella's Millionaire
⑧ The Librarian's Passionate Knight
⑨ Expecting the Sheikh's Baby
⑩ Born To Be Wild
⑪ With Private Eyes
⑫ Passionately Ever After

DYNASTIES: THE BARONES

An extraordinary miniseries featuring the powerful and wealthy Barones of Boston, an elite clan caught in a web of danger, deceit and...desire!

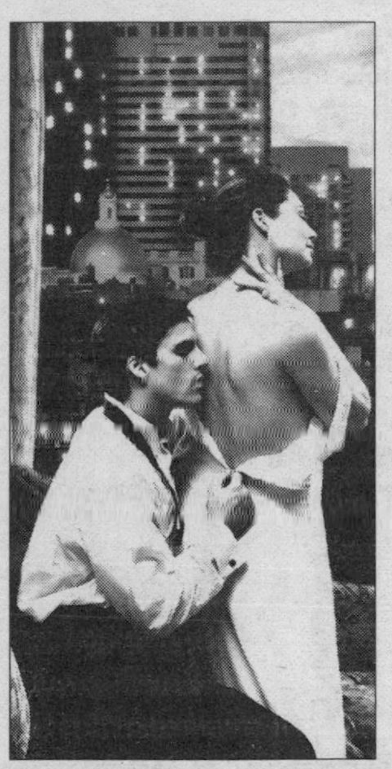

PASSIONATELY EVER AFTER
by Metsy Hingle
(Silhouette Desire #1549)

Discover a love so great—the secret affair between a pregnant Barone beauty and her older, millionaire Conti lover—it can end a long-standing feud and a family curse....

Available December 2003 at your favorite retail outlet.

Visit Silhouette at www.eHarlequin.com SDDYNNPAE

eHARLEQUIN.com

For **FREE online reading,** visit www.eHarlequin.com now and enjoy:

Online Reads
Read **Daily** and **Weekly** chapters from our Internet-exclusive stories by your favorite authors.

Red-Hot Reads
Turn up the heat with one of our more sensual online stories!

Interactive Novels
Cast your vote to help decide how these stories unfold…then stay tuned!

Quick Reads
For shorter romantic reads, try our collection of Poems, Toasts, & More!

Online Read Library
Miss one of our online reads? Come here to catch up!

Reading Groups
Discuss, share and rave with other community members!

For great reading online, visit www.eHarlequin.com today!

INTONL

Your opinion is important to us! Please take a few moments to share your thoughts with us about your experiences with Harlequin and Silhouette books. Your comments will be very useful in ensuring that we deliver books you love to read.

Please take a few minutes to complete the questionnaire, then send it to us at the address below.

Send your completed questionnaires to:
Harlequin/Silhouette Reader Survey, P.O. Box 9046, Buffalo, NY 14269-9046

1. As you may know, there are many different lines under the Harlequin and Silhouette brands. Each of the lines is listed below. Please check the box that most represents your reading habit for each line.

Line	Currently read this line	Do not read this line	Not sure if I read this line
Harlequin American Romance	❑	❑	❑
Harlequin Duets	❑	❑	❑
Harlequin Romance	❑	❑	❑
Harlequin Historicals	❑	❑	❑
Harlequin Superromance	❑	❑	❑
Harlequin Intrigue	❑	❑	❑
Harlequin Presents	❑	❑	❑
Harlequin Temptation	❑	❑	❑
Harlequin Blaze	❑	❑	❑
Silhouette Special Edition	❑	❑	❑
Silhouette Romance	❑	❑	❑
Silhouette Intimate Moments	❑	❑	❑
Silhouette Desire	❑	❑	❑

2. Which of the following best describes why you bought *this book?* One answer only, please.

the picture on the cover	❑	the title	❑
the author	❑	the line is one I read often	❑
part of a miniseries	❑	saw an ad in another book	❑
saw an ad in a magazine/newsletter	❑	a friend told me about it	❑
I borrowed/was given this book	❑	other: ______________	❑

3. Where did you buy *this book?* One answer only, please.

at Barnes & Noble	❑	at a grocery store	❑
at Waldenbooks	❑	at a drugstore	❑
at Borders	❑	on eHarlequin.com Web site	❑
at another bookstore	❑	from another Web site	❑
at Wal-Mart	❑	Harlequin/Silhouette Reader Service/through the mail	❑
at Target	❑		
at Kmart	❑	used books from anywhere	❑
at another department store or mass merchandiser	❑	I borrowed/was given this book	❑

4. On average, how many Harlequin and Silhouette books do you buy at one time?

I buy ______ books at one time ❑
I rarely buy a book ❑

MRQ403SD-1A

5. How many times per month do you shop for any *Harlequin and/or Silhouette* books? One answer only, please.

1 or more times a week	❑	a few times per year	❑
1 to 3 times per month	❑	less often than once a year	❑
1 to 2 times every 3 months	❑	never	❑

6. When you think of your ideal heroine, which *one* statement describes her the best? One answer only, please.

She's a woman who is strong-willed	❑	She's a desirable woman	❑
She's a woman who is needed by others	❑	She's a powerful woman	❑
She's a woman who is taken care of	❑	She's a passionate woman	❑
She's an adventurous woman	❑	She's a sensitive woman	❑

7. The following statements describe types or genres of books that you may be interested in reading. Pick *up to 2 types* of books that you are most interested in.

I like to read about truly romantic relationships ❑
I like to read stories that are sexy romances ❑
I like to read romantic comedies ❑
I like to read a romantic mystery/suspense ❑
I like to read about romantic adventures ❑
I like to read romance stories that involve family ❑
I like to read about a romance in times or places that I have never seen ❑
Other: ________________________________ ❑

The following questions help us to group your answers with those readers who are similar to you. Your answers will remain confidential.

8. Please record your year of birth below.

19 ____

9. What is your marital status?

single ❑ married ❑ common-law ❑ widowed ❑
divorced/separated ❑

10. Do you have children 18 years of age or younger currently living at home?

yes ❑ no ❑

11. Which of the following best describes your employment status?

employed full-time or part-time ❑ homemaker ❑ student ❑
retired ❑ unemployed ❑

12. Do you have access to the Internet from either home or work?

yes ❑ no ❑

13. Have you ever visited eHarlequin.com?
yes ❑ no ❑

14. What state do you live in?

____

15. Are you a member of Harlequin/Silhouette Reader Service?

yes ❑ Account # ____________ no ❑ MRQ403SD-1B

Silhouette®

Desire®

Silhouette Desire's powerful miniseries features six wealthy Texas bachelors—all members of the state's most prestigious club—who set out to unravel the mystery surrounding one tiny baby...and discover true love in the process!

This newest installment continues with

LOCKED UP WITH A LAWMAN
by Laura Wright
(Silhouette Desire #1553)

Meet Clint Andover—a security expert who's sworn off love. When the threats begin, he is determined to protect lovely Tara Roberts—and watch over her night and day. But in keeping Tara out of harm's way, will he risk losing his heart?

Available December 2003 at your favorite retail outlet.

Visit Silhouette at www.eHarlequin.com SDLUWAL

COMING NEXT MONTH

#1549 PASSIONATELY EVER AFTER—Metsy Hingle
Dynasties: The Barones
Dot-com millionaire Steven Conti refused to let a supposed family curse keep him from getting what he wanted: Maria Barone. The dark-haired doe-eyed beauty that had shared his bed, refused to share his life, his home. Now Steven would do anything to get—and keep—the woman who haunted him still.

#1550 SOCIAL GRACES—Dixie Browning
Pampered socialites were a familiar breed to marine archaeologist John Leo MacBride. But Valerie Bonnard, whose father's alleged crimes had wrongly implicated his brother, was not what she appeared. Valerie passionately believed in her father's innocence. And soon John and Valerie were uncovering more than the truth....they were uncovering true passions.

#1551 LONETREE RANCHERS: COLT—Kathie DeNosky
Three years before, Colt Wakefield had broken Kaylee Simpson's heart, leaving heartache and—unknowingly—a baby growing inside her. Now, Colt was back, demanding to get to know his daughter. Kaylee had never been able to resist Colt, but could staying at Lonetree Ranch lead to anything but Kaylee's seduction?

#1552 THORN'S CHALLENGE—Brenda Jackson
A charity calendar needed a photograph of the infamous Thorn Westmoreland to increase its sales. But he would only agree to pose for Tara Matthews in exchange for a week of her exclusive company. If being with each other five minutes had both their hearts racing, how would they survive a week without falling into bed?

#1553 LOCKED UP WITH A LAWMAN—Laura Wright
Texas Cattleman's Club: The Stolen Baby
Clint Andover had been given a simple mission: protect mystery woman Jane Doe and nurse Tara Roberts from an unknown enemy. But that job was proving anything but simple with a stubborn woman like Tara. She challenged him at every turn...and the sparks flying between them became flames that neither could control....

#1554 CHRISTMAS BONUS, STRINGS ATTACHED—Susan Crosby
Behind Closed Doors
Private investigator Nate Caldwell had only hired Lyndsey McCord to pose as his temporary wife for an undercover assignment. Yet, sharing close quarters with the green-eyed temptress had Nate forgetting their marriage was only pretend. Falling for an employee was against company policy...until their passion convinced Nate to change the rules!

SDCNM1103